PRAISE FOR *Nob*

★ "A well-crafted page-turner.... MacColl once again brings a strong female protagonist to life." —*School Library Journal*, starred review

★ "Intriguing.... MacColl skillfully draws from Dickenson's life to create a vision of the young poet as sharp-thinking, nature-obsessed, and determinedly curious." —*Publishers Weekly*, starred review

★ "Suspenseful, often humorous." —*Shelf Awareness for Readers,* starred review

"Plenty of intrigue and suspense . . . a highly imaginative and sensitive heroine in the tradition of Jo March and Anne Shirley." —*The Bulletin of the Center for Children's Books*

PRAISE FOR *Prisoners in the Palace*:

A Junior Library Guild selection
A Kids' Indie Next List selection

★ "A great read."—*School Library Journal*, starred review

"A whip-smart, spunky protagonist and a worthy heroine to root for."
—*Publishers Weekly*

"Fascinating." —*Horn Book Guide*

ALSO BY MICHAELA MACCOLL:

Always Emily
Promise the Night
Prisoners in the Palace

A NOVEL OF INTRIGUE AND ROMANCE BY

MICHAELA MacColl

Nobody's
SECRET

CHRONICLE BOOKS
SAN FRANCISCO

First paperback edition published in 2014. Originally published in hardcover in 2013 by
Chronicle Books LLC.

Copyright © 2013 by Michaela MacColl.

ISBN 978-1-4521-2854-2

The Library of Congress has cataloged the original edition as follows:
Library of Congress Cataloging-in-Publication Data

MacColl, Michaela.
Nobody's secret / by Michaela MacColl.
p. cm.
Summary: When fifteen-year-old Emily Dickinson meets a charming, enigmatic young man
who playfully refuses to tell her his name, she is intrigued—so when he is found dead in her
family's pond in Amherst she is determined to discover his secret, no matter how dangerous
it may prove to be.
ISBN 978-1-4521-0860-5 (alk. paper)
1. Dickinson, Emily, 1830–1886—Juvenile fiction. 2. Women poets, American—19th century—
Juvenile fiction. 3. Amherst (Mass.)—History—19th century—Juvenile fiction. [1. Dickinson,
Emily, 1830–1886—Fiction. 2. Poets—Fiction. 3. Mystery and detective stories. 4. Amherst
(Mass.)—History—19th century—Fiction.] I. Title.
PZ7.M13384No 2013
813.6—dc23
2012030364

Manufactured in China.

Designed by Sara Gillingham.
Typeset in Chronicle Text, No. 1 Type, and Dearest.

10 9 8 7 6 5 4 3 2

Chronicle Books LLC
680 Second Street, San Francisco, California 94107

Chronicle Books—we see things differently. Become part
of our community at www.chroniclebooks.com/teen.

To Rowan, who prefers more crows in her murders

I'm nobody! Who are you?

Are you nobody too?

CHAPTER 1

Emily lay perfectly still, hidden in the tall grass, her eyes closed tight. A chain of wildflowers lay wilted around her neck. But no matter how quiet she was, the bee would not land on her nose. Emily, she told herself sternly, bees are *special*. You can't expect the first one to accept your invitation.

The bee thrummed. A delicate brush of wings tickled her cheek. Pollen drifted into Emily's nose. She sneezed. She didn't need to open her eyes to know that her quarry had flitted away.

The crunch of nearby footsteps made her sigh. Had her mother sent Vinnie to fetch her already? In Mother's view, to play truant from housekeeping was a terrible crime. Especially on laundry day. But this was the first day Emily had felt well enough to wander; she wasn't going home yet. She willed herself to become as invisible as the blur of hummingbirds' wings.

The footsteps came closer. A shadow came between her and the sun. Someone was standing over her. She squeezed her eyes closed even tighter and thought only of the bees.

"A young lady lying hidden among the wildflowers. . . . How unexpected."

Emily's eyes flew open. A young man towered over her. Hastily, she sat up, craning her neck to see him. His silhouette was rimmed with sunlight and his fair hair glistened like strands of fine silk. Her sun-warmed skin suddenly felt chill.

"Hello," she answered warily, glancing toward the stand of white pines that stood between her and home. Then she took a closer look at his fine clothing and her confidence returned. From the high polish on his black shoes and the gold watch peeking from the left pocket of his vest, she could tell he was from a city, perhaps Boston or even New York. He couldn't be more than twenty—twenty-two at the oldest. Harmless, she thought. "Are you a student at the college?"

The college on the hill dominated Amherst's landscape as well as the rhythms of the Dickinson family. Emily's grandfather was one of the founders of Amherst College, and her father was its treasurer.

"I'm no scholar," he said, grimacing. "I've never had any interest in a formal education."

"I'm eager to go to Mount Holyoke Seminary next year." She looked at him curiously, unable to fathom not wanting to learn everything about everything. "I've never met anyone who didn't want to go to school."

"I've been too busy living." He shrugged. "What could I learn in college that I couldn't learn traveling the world?"

The world! Rather than let her envy show on her face, Emily's glance traveled from his well-trimmed hair to his shined shoes. "The civilized parts, I presume."

"I'm off to California as soon as I've finished my business here," he said.

Emily couldn't imagine the courage it would take to go to the wilds of California. "You'll need more rugged clothes if you are going West," she pointed out, gesturing to his tailored coat.

He burst out laughing, but it was a good laugh, not high-pitched and not too hearty.

"May I assist you?" He offered his hand. After a brief hesitation, she put her hand in his. He easily pulled her off the ground. She was small and he was very tall. Her hand lingered on his and for just a moment she could feel the roughness of his skin.

"Your hands prove you aren't a student," she said. "Amherst students rarely work hard enough to callus their hands."

"You're the local expert on college students?" he teased.

"I know all of them," she sighed. "My father is . . . connected with the College."

To her pleasure, the stranger didn't seem interested in her father. As if it were of no importance, he asked, "What were you doing down there, anyway?"

She paused, considering his intelligent eyes. Finally, she told the bald truth without explanation: "Hoping a bee would land on my nose."

He nodded, as though that made all the sense in the world. The silence lengthened while Emily waited for the inevitable question. Finally she said, "You aren't going to ask me why?"

He pursed his lips. "I suspect you want to know what it feels like."

His easy understanding was like a blow to the body. She nodded, speechless.

"But aren't you afraid of being stung?" he asked.

"I don't know. It hasn't happened yet." She paused. "But I'm sure it will be excruciating."

His forehead crinkled and his mouth twisted to stop a smile. "And that's a good thing?"

"It's a new experience. If you are sequestered at home, as I am, new experiences are to be savored."

"Perhaps you'll be lucky," he said. "I have a relation who keeps bees. He doesn't even notice the beestings."

"I'm very sensitive to natural poisons," Emily assured him. "Of all the girls in my botany class, I reacted most to poison oak. So if I'm stung, it's bound to be painful. But I still hope a bee will visit."

"You've picked a good spot," he said, "with all these wildflowers about."

"So far the bees have decided my nose is not the place for them." She picked a long blade of grass from her braid of red hair and smoothed her dark cotton skirt. It was short, showing several inches above her ankle. Her mother scolded her daily to wear longer dresses that were appropriate to her fifteen years. Emily usually chose the shorter dress that permitted free movement, but today she wished she had listened to her mother.

"Lavender is a favorite for bees." He looked around and spied a purple bush. He pulled a sprig from it and handed it to her. "Try this."

She secreted his offering in her pocket. "And whom do I have the pleasure of thanking for my gift?"

He started to introduce himself, then seemed to think better of it. "I'm nobody important." He grinned, revealing a mouth of straight teeth. "Who are you?"

Emily paused. She was the eldest daughter of one of the town fathers and everyone knew her name. But this stranger didn't.

How dreary to be somebody all the time, she thought. Feeling very mischievous, she said, "I'm nobody too."

"Hello, Miss Nobody," he said with an inclination of his head. "Do you live around here?"

She nodded. "Just beyond that stand of white pines." Harmless as he might appear, it wouldn't hurt for him to know that her home and family were close.

"It's a pleasing spot. Amherst always was a pretty town."

"You aren't from around here." It wasn't a question.

"I've visited Amherst before," he said, "but I don't belong anywhere." The gleam in his eye forbade her to pity him. After a moment, he asked, "How old are you?"

"Almost sixteen," she said.

"So fifteen," he said, but in such a genial way Emily didn't take offense. "And why aren't you in school, if it's so important? Are you playing truant?"

"I go to Amherst Academy. It's just up the road off the Common, but we're between terms right now."

"And you're free to frolic with the bees? No chores at home calling out for you to do?"

She couldn't meet his eyes.

"I don't blame you, Miss Nobody," he said. "I ran away from home to be free from what was expected of me."

"I'll go home soon," she said. "But only when the washing is finished!"

"Much better to make friends with bees." He looked around thoughtfully. "But if you're fifteen—excuse me, almost sixteen—you're old enough to know that if you really want to attract a bee, you need to be sweeter."

Emily felt a hint of a blush on her cheeks. "My family is always complaining of my prickly disposition," she agreed.

"I'm sure that's not true." He bowed gallantly. "I meant you must taste of summer. That's what a bee wants. Close your eyes."

Emily pursed her lips, considering him and his odd request. His open visage reassured her, and with hardly any reluctance she did as he asked.

"Oh!" she said, stepping back in surprise. He had dabbed her nose with a sticky substance. She opened her eyes and saw that he held a chunk of oozing honeycomb in his right hand.

"This will summon every bee in the township." His eyebrows lifted, almost daring her to take offense.

"We'll have to see, won't we, Mr. Nobody?" Emily crossed her eyes to catch a glimpse of her nose.

"I'll leave you to it," he said. "I must be going now."

"To California?"

"Soon. First I have to take care of some family business." His genial mood disappeared like a shadow at high noon. He folded his honeycomb back in the handkerchief. She noticed a monogram with a bold "JW" embroidered with black silk thread. "Some unpleasant accounts need to be settled."

"Sometimes we have to endure unpleasantness to do the right thing," Emily agreed, recalling more than one such occasion. "It's often inconvenient."

"Unavoidable, in this case." His voice had an edge belied by his gentle manner. "But unpleasantness is the last thing a pretty girl like you should worry about."

Emily's forthright nature couldn't allow such an untruth to stand. "I'm not pretty," she said, matter-of-factly, as if it did not bother her at all. "I'm the plain sister."

"How refreshing to meet such modesty, but I think it's misplaced."

Another item to add to his list of good qualities; he thought she was pretty. She crinkled her nose, wishing it wasn't dotted with freckles. "That's very kind of you, but I think you flatter me."

"Better to flatter than to wound. That's always been my maxim." He pulled out his pocket watch, a gold affair with a "W" engraved on its back. His face displayed his consternation. "It's getting late. Good luck with your bee hunting."

"Thank you," she said. "Have a good day, Mr. Nobody."

"And you, Miss Nobody!" With a wave, he turned and strode away, disappearing into the hazy sunshine. Staring after him, she dabbed at her nose with a fingertip and licked it. The honey was full of clover, honeysuckle, and green apples, made by bees with discriminating taste. The hive must be nearby for the honey to be so fresh. Emily wished she had asked Mr. Nobody where to find it.

She lay down in the grass, arranging her body straight and comfortable. Mr. Nobody's honey was indeed the missing catalyst for her experiment. Only moments later, a large bee landed on her nose. Eyes closed, Emily concentrated on every detail. The vibration of the buzzing tickled her nostrils. She felt certain she could count each one of the bee's six legs. Its fur smelled of flowers. And all the while, her body quivered, wanting to flee before the sting.

Some keep the Sabbath going to church;

I keep it, staying at home

CHAPTER 2

Rain streamed down the windows. Translucent trails marked their passing like prison bars. A comfortable prison to be sure, Emily had to admit, with soft chairs arranged for conversation and needlework and books close at hand.

She arranged the sprig of lavender just so in the center of the flower press and screwed down the glass plate to flatten the flower. When it was ready, she would put it in her most private of notebooks.

Emily already knew what she would write in memory of her meeting with the mysterious Mr. Nobody:

There is a flower that Bees prefer.

She didn't know which words would follow yet, but doubtless they would come to her.

With a sigh, she leaned her forehead against the windowpane, straining to make out the graveyard on the far side of the garden. On the whole, the Dickinsons were very fond of their home on North Pleasant Street with its ample rooms, wide-planked floors, and large, light-filled kitchen, but only Emily counted the graveyard as one of the house's assets. She enjoyed walking up the gentle rise to commune with its inhabitants, who were all but forgotten except for the names on tombstones, eroded by wind and weather. One of her favorite places to sit and think was at the spring-fed pond at the edge of their property that adjoined the cemetery. But not in the pouring rain, and not with Mother so suspicious.

"Emily Elizabeth Dickinson, stop staring out the window. You aren't going anywhere—not after you abandoned your sister yesterday!" Her mother was wrapped in quilts. Mrs. Dickinson half-closed her eyes, trying to ward off one of her devastating headaches.

"Mama, it's all right," protested Vinnie from her position in the armchair next to the small fire, a purring tomcat on her lap and *Godey's Lady's Book,* her favorite fashion magazine, in her hand. As Emily had hinted to Mr. Nobody, Vinnie was the pretty sister, full of health and blessed with an easy disposition. Almost three years younger than Emily, she was already more popular at school. Her chestnut hair was thick and lush. Mrs. Dickinson had only recently let her begin to grow it out. "I didn't mind doing Emily's share."

Emily snorted. Vinnie had indeed minded, and had told Emily so in no uncertain terms the night before in their shared bedroom. But the Dickinson children always honored their alliance against their parents, much to the dismay of their mother.

"Nevertheless, it was unfair of Emily," Mrs. Dickinson continued. "Today she has to make up for it. Have you finished dusting?"

"Yes, Mother." Emily hastily retrieved the discarded dust cloth and rubbed at the window sash without conviction.

"And you've polished the tables?"

"Yes, Mother," Emily said. Under her breath she whispered, "All the pestilence is swept away."

"Very well." Mrs. Dickinson was holding the *Hampshire Gazette,* the family's preferred local paper. "I see your father's business card is prominently displayed on the front page."

Emily came to look over her shoulder.

Edward Dickinson
Commissioner in Bankruptcy,
Master in Chancery, Attorney
Amherst, Ma

"It looks very distinguished," Emily said.

Mrs. Dickinson's eyes were already moving down the page. "More news about potatoes. Our potatoes were fine; I don't see this blight they keep writing about."

Emily and Vinnie exchanged glances. Their mother was quite capable of ignoring anything that didn't directly touch her home or family.

"Girls, listen to this." Mrs. Dickinson began to read from her favorite part of the newspaper, the Miscellany, where humorous and tragic stories were collected from all over the country. "It's from Greenville, South Carolina."

Horrors of Hydrophobia: The Greenville (S.C.) Moun-taineer states that a slave in that vicinity, owned by Mr. Hiram Cosley, was bitten by a mad dog a few days ago. . . . Two of Mr. Cosley's sons took a gun and went out for the purpose of finding and killing him. They had proceeded some distance from the house without finding him, when the younger brother (12 or 14 years of age,) started back leaving the gun with his brother. Before reaching the house he met the dog, which instantly sprang upon him, lacerating the back part of the neck in a shocking manner. The dog was killed, but the agony of the youth, both in mind and body, was distressing in the extreme. He begged his father to shoot him, and thereby avoid the horrid death of hydrophobia, which he supposed awaited him.

Vinnie had displaced the cat to move closer to the edge of her seat and Emily was pacing as though the suspense were chasing her about the room. Mrs. Dickinson stopped reading.

"Well?" Emily said. "What happened? Did he go mad?"

"Did the boy's father shoot him?" Vinnie asked.

Mrs. Dickinson shrugged. "The story stops there."

"That's not an ending!" Emily cried with frustration.

Mrs. Dickinson carefully folded up the newspaper and put it aside. "The ending isn't as important as the lesson. You'll recall I've always told you to stay away from strange dogs."

There was a knock at the door.

"I'll answer it," Emily said, exasperated. A moment later she returned, holding a folded square of paper. "Our neighbor, Mr. Banbury, did us the courtesy of bringing our post. There's a letter from Father."

"But we heard from him only yesterday," Mrs. Dickinson said, taking the letter. "I hope nothing has happened in Boston. Perhaps his baggage has been lost?"

"Mother, he's been at the hotel for three days. If his baggage were to go astray, it would have happened by now," Emily said.

"I hate when he travels," Mrs. Dickinson said. "Why would anyone want to leave home?"

"Mama, what does he say?" Vinnie asked, sounding almost as anxious as her mother.

"I don't dare read it," Mrs. Dickinson said. "What if it is bad news?"

"Oh, for heaven's sakes, Mother! I'll do it!" Emily took the letter from her mother's hands. Her strong fingers made quick work of the wax seal that kept the letter private as it traveled through the mail.

Dearest Wife,

I am writing because I forgot to mention that Jasper needs to be reshod this week. Please send Emily or Vinnie with him to the blacksmith. Take him to Mr. Magee in the center of town (not the smith on the north side of town). Remind our daughters that Jasper kicks. And when they lead him on the road, have them beware of any loud noises that might make the horse rear up and knock them down. They should stay to watch the blacksmith to ensure he replaces every shoe with new ones, but they must avoid breathing in the fumes from the smithy. I know you will not fail me. Do not worry overmuch, it is not good for your health.

With love,
Edward

Emily pressed her palm to her lips to stifle a chuckle. Her father's letters were always the same. Don't shirk your duty, no matter how perilous. Don't endanger yourself, despite the risks that are all around us. And above all, don't be anxious.

Vinnie and their mother looked relieved.

"If your father wants this done, we must do it immediately," Mrs. Dickinson said. "Vinnie, you are better with animals. You should go."

"But Mother, it's raining!"

"I'll go." Emily knelt by her mother's side. "I owe it to Vinnie for leaving her yesterday with all the chores."

Vinnie snorted.

"Emily, you've only just recovered your health," Mrs. Dickinson said. Emily had missed several weeks of school because of a persistent cough. Dr. Gridley, the family physician, had worried that it might be consumption. The dreaded disease had claimed many of Mrs. Dickinson's relations, and she lived in fear that it would descend upon her children.

"I've been fine for almost a week. The fresh air will be good for me."

Mrs. Dickinson glanced from her husband's letter to the rain outside. Her face pinched with anxiety, she stroked Emily's hand. "You'll be careful?"

"Of course, Mother." Emily jumped to her feet and took her cloak from its hook in the hall.

Vinnie followed with a scarf to wrap around Emily's hair. "Don't think I don't know how you long to get out of this house," she whispered.

"Would you rather go?" Emily said. At Vinnie's involuntary glance toward her warm chair, Emily laughed. "I thought so. You're worse than your cats. You don't like getting wet." Before her mother or sister could reconsider, Emily ducked out into the drizzle and picked her way across the mud to the small stable.

"Hello, Jasper," she said, patting the horse on its withers. He skittered in his stall and tossed his head before she clipped a rope to his halter. "You're bored to death, aren't you? I can sympathize!"

With her father's warnings about Jasper in mind, Emily avoided being trampled or knocked down as she led the horse out of the yard to head up the long incline toward the Common, the grassy square that formed the heart of Amherst. The mud made for tough going, but she was in no hurry to return home.

The drizzle became a downpour and Emily could barely see a yard ahead of her. She turned into the alley behind the row of merchants in the Common.

"Hello, Miss Emily," the blacksmith said from his usual place by the hot stove. His body was shaped like a barrel, and his legs didn't seem thick enough to support his weight. Shining with perspiration, he wielded a red-hot poker like a sword. To Emily's amused eye, he seemed to be steaming in the damp air.

"Mr. Magee, how are you today?"

"Not too bad, for all that my rheumatism is bothering me a bit."

"I'm sorry to have added to your labors, but my father would like Jasper reshod."

"There's one client in front of you. If you would be so kind, put Jasper in my extra stall next door. I'll bring him back to your house for you."

Thinking of her stuffy home, Emily said quickly, "I don't mind waiting. I might go to the bookstore."

He shrugged. "If you please, but be sure to tell your father I offered."

Emily tugged on Jasper's bridle to lead him back out to the extra stall. The rain, now a fine mist, felt cool and refreshing after the stifling heat of the smith's forge. Without warning, Jasper, who had been a model of good behavior until then, balked at entering the narrow stall. She tugged and pulled, but nothing would persuade him to go inside.

"I bet you would go if Vinnie asked," she muttered, slapping the horse's flank. Jasper neighed and reared up, jerking the rope out of her hands.

"May I be of assistance, Miss Nobody?" A voice from behind her made her jump.

She stumbled backward and would have fallen except for the pair of strong arms that caught her.

"Mr. Nobody?" She recovered her balance. Almost reluctantly, she extricated herself from his grasp.

"I saw you from across the Common and thought I would come and renew our acquaintance." He stepped forward. He was wearing oilskins that fit his tall frame as if they were cut for him. Hatless, his golden hair was dark with rain and plastered to his head. He shook out his coat and water splashed off in every direction. Drops clung to the blond stubble on his chin.

Emily smoothed her damp hair and wiped the moisture from her face. Even though she did not look her best, she was pleased to meet him again and said so.

Mr. Nobody stepped forward and took Jasper's halter. "May I?" he asked politely.

"I would be grateful. The beast is more stubborn than . . . than . . ." Emily would normally have finished the sentence with a comparison to herself, but she was loath to say so to him.

"Than a mule?" he asked, eyes twinkling, almost as though he knew what she was thinking.

"Nothing so commonplace," she protested, but she couldn't think of anything better.

"There's a secret to dealing with a stubborn beast," he said. "Turn him around." He led Jasper so that his hind-quarters were facing the doorway. Without hesitating, the horse backed into the stall.

"Good boy," Mr. Nobody said, rubbing the horse's long nose.

"That's a useful trick," Emily said.

He nodded thoughtfully. "Sometimes you need to attack a problem from a different direction."

Emily remembered he had spoken about accounts needing to be settled. "Are you reconsidering how to tackle your dilemma?" she asked.

"I thought I knew what I was going to do, but there might be a kinder way. After all, family is family, no matter what their crimes." He pulled a silver flask out of his pocket. He offered it to her, but wasn't surprised when she refused.

Mr. Nobody took a small sip; Emily could smell the brandy in the air, blending with the dust from the hay and the pungent smell of wet horse.

Crimes? "What did your family do?" Emily asked with an avid curiosity she didn't try to conceal.

"I can't say yet—I need to be certain of my facts. But if I'm right, there's hell to pay . . . and perhaps a little fun to be had. Lord knows that my family deserves to be taught a lesson." He shook himself. Jasper snorted and shivered in the same way. Emily turned away to hide her grin.

"Families are oftentimes unaccountable," Emily said. "Mine doesn't understand me in the least. Mother is afraid of the world outside, so her highest ambition for me is to be a perfect housekeeper, like her. She had a fine education, but . . . "

"I thought you said an education was all a girl needed?" he teased.

"I didn't say that exactly," Emily said. "In Mother's case, it's been a complete waste. She avoids any sort of argument or discussion about philosophy."

"What about your father? You said he was with the College."

"Father's no better," Emily retorted. "He buys me books all the time, but tells me not to read them."

"Why not?" Mr. Nobody leaned forward, eager for the answer.

"They might put ideas in my head," she said slyly.

"Too late for that!" He threw back his head and laughed. "Miss Nobody," he cried, "what a fortunate happenstance that I encountered you. I needed to laugh today."

A smile played on Emily's lips. "I did, too," she said, tucking a loose strand of hair into her bonnet. "Mr. Nobody, I've been thinking about our talk yesterday. You said you preferred travel to education. Why?"

He looked puzzled. "To see what's next, I suppose. To reach to the next horizon. Why do you ask?"

"I love my home and hate venturing far from Amherst. But how can I make a mark on a world I never visit?"

He leaned against a wooden pillar that held up a loft stuffed to the brim with bales of hay. A shower of gold dust floated down around his head, creating a halo. "What kind of mark do you want to make?"

Emily hesitated. She had kept her secret from her family and friends, but it would be so easy to tell him. "I like to write . . . poems," she said in a low voice.

MICHAELA MACCOLL

"A lady poet." He considered it. "I look forward to seeing your work in print. 'An Ode to a Stubborn Gelding,' by Miss Nobody."

"Publish?" Emily took a step backward and bumped against Jasper's side. "I couldn't do that!" Her skin crawled at the thought of strangers reading her little poems.

"Miss Nobody, don't worry." He reached over and stroked her hand. His touch burned and soothed at the same time. "Just write about adventures you have here at home. Later you can worry about publishing."

As he spoke, there was a break in the dreariness of the rain. A vista opened through the alley into the Common. "If I'm to finish my business, I have to go. Perhaps you can direct me to the law offices of Mr. Dickinson?" He ran a hand over his wet hair.

Emily went very still. "Why?"

"He handled some business for my family," he explained.

She relaxed. "He's away trying a case in Boston," she said, "but his office is above the Graves and Fields store, opposite the hotel."

"You're very well informed," he said. "Tell me, does he have a good reputation? Is he honest?"

"Of course he is!" Emily's voice was raised.

He stepped back, holding up his hands in mock surrender. "It was a question only, Miss Nobody."

Emily realized if Mr. Nobody was one of her father's clients, her chances of remaining anonymous were slim. "He's my father. My name is Emily Dickinson," she admitted.

Every aspect of his face expressed his dismay. "Please accept my apology. I had no intention of insulting your father." Putting his hands to his heart, he entreated her to forgive him.

Emily inclined her head with mock solemnity. "Your apology is accepted."

"I like how loyal you are, though . . . family should stand together." The timbre of his voice shifted from penitence to something harder. Emily wasn't sure what to make of it.

"My father or not," Emily said, "let me assure you that there isn't a more honest man in the entire state of Massachusetts."

"A testimonial I am happy to accept." He gestured toward the law offices. "Is there anyone in the office to help me?"

"His clerk, Mr. Ripley, should be there." Emily hesitated and then said, "But don't tell him you know me, please."

"Why not? I'm quite proud of our acquaintance."

Feeling his charm all over again, her eyes dropped to stare at the tops of her muddy boots. "Amherst is like a small pond. Everyone proclaims their business to the rest of the bog. No one needs to know about our friendship."

"As you wish," he said, taking no offense. "I'll be on my way."

"Wait," Emily said. "I've told you my name. What is yours?"

"I prefer being mysterious," he said, with a slightly wicked smile.

Emily scowled, but proffered her hand. "I'm very grateful for your help with Jasper." He shook her hand with great solemnity. "I hope some day to return the favor."

"I'm interested in this college of yours," he said. "Perhaps you would show me around when the weather improves? Tomorrow?"

Emily glanced up the hill to where the First Congregational Church was situated. "I would like to, very much, but tomorrow is Sunday. I'll be in church for most of the day."

"What a shame," Mr. Nobody said. "I love my God as much as the next person, but I find it hard to spend hours on a beautiful summer morning in his house on a hard bench."

She nodded without realizing it. "Our family box pew is in the very front of the church, and when my father pulls the door shut, I feel so ... trapped."

"Like a rabbit in a snare," he said.

"Wouldn't it be lovely," Emily exclaimed, "if we could worship wherever we wished?"

Mr. Nobody squinted as though he were looking toward a faraway place. "I would pray at sea," he said. "I never appreciated God's accomplishments until I sailed the ocean. That horizon has no limits."

"I've never seen the sea, only the harbor at Boston," Emily admitted. "I'm partial to meadows."

At that moment, the church bell tolled the hour. Mr. Nobody said, "Instead of a bell calling you to worship, we could have a . . . "

"A bobolink!" Emily supplied her favorite bird. "And the sermons would never be too long."

"Amen," he said, and they both laughed.

"Perhaps Monday?" he asked wistfully.

"But I thought you were headed West?" Emily asked.

He nodded. "If I adopt my new plan of action, I may stay for several days."

"I'd be honored to give you a tour," Emily said, proud that she kept her delight in check and out of her voice. "Meet me at nine o'clock at the church up the hill, next to the College."

"I look forward to it." With a jaunty wave, he disappeared into the mist.

"As do I," Emily whispered after him.

The stray ships passing spied a face
Upon the waters borne,
With eyes in death still begging raised,
And hands beseeching thrown.

CHAPTER 3

Monday morning dawned bright and glistening. Emily was sitting near the kitchen window overlooking the pond. Squinting in the light, she wrote furiously in her notebook. Her conversation with Mr. Nobody about alternate means of worship had been reverberating in her head, like a moth trapped in a lantern. It seemed impossible that only two days ago she had been standing in the pouring rain with him. Or that she would see him again in just a few minutes.

"How many times do I need to ask you to do your chores?" her mother asked from the doorway. "Shouldn't you be churning the butter?"

Emily could hear one of Mother's "bad turns" announcing itself, and the muscles in the back of her neck tightened. When Mother was ill, her daughters' plans were of no account.

As though she were trying to catch a wisp of smoke in her fist, Emily saw her plans with Mr. Nobody were in jeopardy. Shoving her notebook deep in her skirt pocket, Emily rushed to placate her mother, who had settled in her customary rocking chair at the stove.

Emily's arm knew how to churn butter without supervision, so her mind was free to wander. With each crank of the paddle, she unpacked another detail of her meetings with Mr. Nobody. She glanced across the table to where Vinnie was making a cake. Although she was inclined to confide in her sister, Emily had kept the handsome stranger a secret. Vinnie would tease her, or ask sensible questions Emily didn't want to answer. Or, worse, Vinnie would want to join them this morning—and Emily couldn't bear it if Mr. Nobody preferred Vinnie to herself.

"Is the butter ready yet?" her mother interrupted. Emily was pleased to hear that her voice sounded a bit stronger.

"Almost," Emily said, her shoulders aching from churning the paddle in the thickened cream. "I wish we could just buy the butter ready-made like Abiah Root's family does."

Her mother snorted. Emily and Vinnie exchanged grins at the unladylike sound.

"After all, we can afford butter from the shop," Emily said.

"'Tis wasteful when we can do it ourselves."

"But..."

Mrs. Dickinson shook her head. "Emily, it doesn't matter that we have the means now. Store-bought butter is an extravagance. When I was just married, I had to take in boarders to make ends meet. I don't know what I would have done without Mrs. Child's book to help me economize."

Emily's sigh was echoed by Vinnie's exhaled breath. Mrs. Child's opus, *The American Frugal Housewife,* had haunted their domestic hours since they were babes.

Mrs. Dickinson, ignoring her daughters' exasperation, paraphrased: "'Convenience should be a secondary object to economy.'"

"'Economy is a poor man's revenue,'" Vinnie continued. When Emily failed to chime in, Vinnie jabbed her in the side with a floury elbow.

"'And extravagance a rich man's ruin,'" Emily said so quickly that the words ran together like the egg whites in Vinnie's batter. "But wouldn't baking day be a pleasure if we could just scoop in the butter we needed? Without churning for hours and hours?" She held up her hands to display angry red creases on her palms from the wooden paddle.

"Next, you'll want to buy our flour without a visit to the mill," Vinnie teased, as she began working the ingredients together in her favorite bowl. It was the precise hue of a robin's egg. "And get our spices already ground."

"There are so many better ways to spend our time!" Emily said.

"And what would they be?" asked her mother. "Disappearing for hours on end? Staring at flowers? Scribbling in your mysterious notebooks? Now that the school term is finished, your time is best spent learning to bake for the family table. You too, Vinnie. Mind you don't forget the cinnamon." She came to Emily's side to check the butter. Emily stepped back and stumbled across a streak of dark fur.

"Vinnie—that cat of yours!" Emily cried.

"Be careful, Emily!" Vinnie knelt down and scooped up the gray tabby. As she draped it around her shoulders, the cat's loud purr filled the kitchen. "She's still nursing. Her nerves are in a fragile state."

"That's no excuse for always being underfoot." Emily sniffed. "When are those kittens going to the barn?"

Shooting Emily a reproachful glance, Vinnie said, "They aren't ready yet." As if on cue, the three oversized kittens began mewing in the basket near the stove. "The nights are too cold."

"It's August, young lady," Mrs. Dickinson corrected. "The nights are warm enough that your precious kittens can sleep in the barn." She held Vinnie's rebellious glance until Vinnie nodded. "And wash your hands. Who knows where that beast has been?"

"Just outside, playing with the toads and crickets," Vinnie said.

Mrs. Dickinson scowled and handed Vinnie a towel and the box of soap powder.

"Mother," Emily began, hoping to take advantage of her mother's distraction. "I need to go into town at nine o'clock. I have to meet a friend."

"Who?"

Before Emily could present her carefully prepared story, a scream pierced the air outside. Emily was instantly out the door, Vinnie hard on her heels.

Their occasional daily help, Mary Katherine, was standing outside the chicken coop, a mess of broken eggshells and yolks at her feet. She was still shrieking.

"For goodness' sake, what is it?" Emily cried. "Did Vinnie's black cat cross your path again?" Mary Katherine's Irish superstitions were both infuriating and a source of amusement to the family.

Vinnie was gentler and put her arms around the girl to comfort her. "Mary Katherine, what's wrong?"

Trembling, the maid opened her mouth, but no sound came out.

Emily reproached herself for speaking so sharply; the girl was in great distress. "What's happened?" she asked in a kinder voice.

Mary Katherine lifted her arm and pointed toward the pond at the far end of the garden.

Emily and Vinnie stared where she indicated, and for a moment they were frozen in horror. A man was floating facedown in the water among the lily pads, drifting under the trees on the opposite side of the pond.

Vinnie inhaled sharply, and her breath made a whooping sound that quickened Emily's pulse. She ran to the water's edge, Vinnie not far behind. The graceful branches of a weeping willow caressed the man's back in the light breeze. His coat floated above his head and obscured the color of his hair.

"Look at that mess!" Mrs. Dickinson cried from the kitchen doorway. "A waste of perfectly good eggs."

"Mother, there's a dead man in our pond!" Vinnie called out.

"Nonsense." Mrs. Dickinson didn't budge. "Mary Katherine is imagining things."

"Mother, Vinnie and I see the body too!" Emily said over her shoulder.

"Oh." Mrs. Dickinson put out her hand to support herself against the doorjamb. "Are you sure he's really dead?"

Vinnie and Emily looked at each other and then at the still body.

"He's dead," they said together.

Emily started to circle the pond, trying to get a clearer view of the unfortunate man.

"Emily, get back!" Mrs. Dickinson cried, her voice faint.

Emily halted. "Mother, I have to see who it is!"

Mrs. Dickinson's breath came fast and shallow. "A dead man is no sight for a young lady. Girls, come inside!" she cried.

Vinnie hissed, "Emily, don't upset Mother!"

"Maybe we know him. We have to look," Emily urged.

Vinnie looked from Emily to her mother and back again. "Mother needs us." She tugged at her sister's sleeve.

Reluctantly, Emily trailed Vinnie back to the house.

"We need to fetch the constable," Mrs. Dickinson said.

"He might be anywhere," Emily said. "I can find Reverend Colton."

"Yes, he will know what to do," her mother began. "Wait." She reached out and grabbed Emily's chin so she could look her daughter in the eyes. "Emily, you look overexcited. You might start coughing at any moment. Vinnie, run and get Reverend Colton." She held the door. "We'll wait inside."

"But . . ." Emily protested.

"You aren't strong enough for such exertions," Mrs. Dickinson said. "No arguments."

Vinnie, eyes wide, ran off without another word.

"I need to sit down." Mary Katherine stumbled toward a chair.

"Mary Katherine, stop crying." Mrs. Dickinson sank into a chair next to her, shooting the maid a sour look. "I'm sure it was upsetting, but it's over now. Reverend Colton will take care of it. We won't be involved."

Emily stood at the window, staring toward the pond. "Mother, of course we're involved. Whoever the poor soul is—was—he died in our pond."

"Stop saying that!" Mrs. Dickinson groaned and put her head in her hands. "I wish your father were here. Or Austin."

With a sigh, Emily filled the kettle with water and put it on the stove to boil.

Mary Katherine's sobs were reduced to a few hiccoughs. Her dark hair hung in a cloud about her head. She stood up, her tall figure dwarfing Emily's. "Miss, I'm sorry for making such a spectacle of myself."

"So you should be, silly girl," Emily said, not unkindly. "Here, sit down and churn the butter; that will calm your nerves." Under her breath she said, "It always deadens mine."

Gulping, Mary Katherine nodded. Emily left her to it and went back to the window, craning her neck to see. Mrs. Dickinson drank her tea without saying a word, watching Emily keenly.

As they waited for Vinnie to return, the clock struck nine. No sooner did Emily edge toward the door than her mother said, "No, Emily."

"But . . . "

"Emily, you are not to go out there."

The minute hand continued until it reached the half-hour mark and Emily gave up all hope of making her assignation. What would Mr. Nobody think if she failed to keep their appointment? Of course, once he learned why, he would forgive her, but what if she never saw him again to explain? If only Mother would let her go for just a few minutes.

At the sound of footsteps, she jumped up. Vinnie, flushed with running, came back into the kitchen.

"I did it, Mother. The reverend is here to take the body away." She pointed outside. Reverend Colton and a handful of men were trudging toward the pond.

"Did you see anything more?" Emily whispered.

"Me? You were here. What did you see?"

"Nothing." Emily bit her lower lip. "If only Mother wasn't so afraid of everything, I could have gone out there."

"Who do you think he is?" Vinnie asked. "What do you think happened?"

Glancing over at her mother's stiff-backed figure, Emily answered, "He was dressed like a working man." It was the first thing she had noticed. "Probably a tramp."

"Mother's always warning us about drowning in that pond."

"They're coming," Mary Katherine said, a tremor in her voice.

Without a word, they went to the door to see. Reverend Colton, his face solemn, supervised a procession of men, carrying a man-shaped burden covered by a plain cloth. He saw Mrs. Dickinson and hurried over, telling his men to wait. "Mrs. Dickinson, Emily, Lavinia."

"Thank you for coming so quickly," Mrs. Dickinson said.

"It's a shame that your family has been bothered. I hope you aren't too distressed."

"Of course I'm distressed. He had no business dying in our pond." Mrs. Dickinson's voice was accusing.

"Mother, I doubt he was worried about inconveniencing the Dickinsons when he drowned," Emily said sharply.

Vinnie giggled nervously, but fell silent when her mother glared at her.

"Emily, Vinnie, be still," her mother said. "What will Reverend Colton think of you?"

The reverend turned his wise gray eyes to Emily. "Only that your charming daughters have been protected from the tragic side of life." He sighed heavily. "I've attended too many deaths to make light of any. Especially when the poor gentleman is such a mystery. I've never seen him before."

"Was he a *gentleman*?" Emily asked.

Mrs. Dickinson brushed the question aside. "Do we know if the poor man died in a state of grace?"

Her mother's preoccupation with the hereafter had never failed to irritate Emily. Who cared about that when the here and now was so much more interesting? She stamped her right foot. "Mother, before we worry about his soul, don't you think he deserves a name?"

"Emily! That is none of your concern."

Before Emily could draw breath to retort, the reverend rested a hand on Mrs. Dickinson's arm. "My dear lady, until we identify the poor man, he is the responsibility of every good Christian in Amherst."

Emily rewarded him with a cautious smile.

"How will you find out who he is?" Vinnie asked.

"After Dr. Gridley has taken a look at the body, we'll lay out the poor man in the vestry of the Meeting House. Someone must know him."

Mrs. Dickinson stepped back, her hand at her throat. "Are you sure that's wise? My husband might not approve. That man could be . . . anyone." She glanced about, as though Mr. Dickinson might suddenly appear from Boston. "And you can't leave him there for long."

"The church's basement is cool enough, Mother," Emily said. "He won't smell for a few days."

"Emily!"

Staring at the ground, Emily mumbled an apology. Vinnie grabbed her hand and squeezed it. When Emily glanced up, she saw her sister holding her breath, trying not to laugh.

The reverend was also struggling to keep a straight face. "With good fortune, someone will recognize him before we need to worry about . . . " He coughed. "Nature taking its course." He paused, then went on. "We've sent for the constable. He'll have some questions for you."

"All of us?" Emily asked, unable to keep the pleasure out of her voice.

"Why would he?" her mother asked in the same moment. "We know nothing of this unfortunate tragedy."

"Of course you don't," Reverend Colton assured, "but he must do his duty and ask whether you heard or saw anything."

"Duty must be done, I suppose," Mrs. Dickinson muttered. "I hope his questions are brief. I don't want the girls to be further upset by this inconvenience."

The reverend's eyebrows rose, but he said nothing. He took his leave, and his men hoisted their burden to bring the body to the church.

"We should go," Vinnie said. "Perhaps we'll recognize him."

"It's our duty," Emily said.

"Absolutely not! Emily, Lavinia, I forbid either of you to do such a thing."

Emily spied the reverend leaving the garden by the side gate. With a mental nod to Mr. Nobody's wisdom, Emily decided to approach the problem from a different direction. She ran out of the kitchen to look out the parlor window, hoping to get a better view of the grisly parade.

"Emily!" her mother called. "Don't you dare. The reverend will think you are morbid."

From the parlor, Emily couldn't see clearly; an elm blocked her line of sight. Ignoring her mother, she took the stairs two at a time and ran into the room she shared with Vinnie. Looking down at the procession, she could only see a body dressed in cheap, ill-fitting clothing. His face was covered. She could have screamed in frustration. Who was he?

There's been a death in the opposite house

As lately as to-day

I know it by the numb look

Such houses have alway.

CHAPTER 4

At her first opportunity to slip out, Emily made a beeline for the pond. She left Mrs. Dickinson dozing fitfully on the sofa. As for Vinnie, she was too engrossed in cutting a new dress pattern to spare a thought for Emily.

Emily studied the scene for a long time. When the reverend's men had removed the body, they had left a swath of lily pads ripped from the roots. Because of the rain the day before, there were too many footprints on the muddy bank to tell her what happened.

She moved around the pond, ducking under the willow branches and pushing bushes aside. She noticed an area on the far side of the pond where the mud was particularly churned. She clambered up the bank, slipping in the slick dirt to where the road passed closest to the pond.

"I bet this is where he went in," she murmured. "But it was chilly last night; I remember Vinnie fussing about the cats. He wouldn't have gone swimming. Perhaps he fell in?"

She cast her eye over the ground and spied a fresh trace of carriage wheels in the mud. She knelt down, heedless of the dirt on her gray skirt. Her nose almost to the ground, she examined the track. It was narrow, and within the groove of the right wheel she spied an odd square imprint, as though the wheel had been repaired with a thumb-sized block of wood.

She pulled a small notebook from its hiding place inside her corset. A length of stiff whalebone was supposed to go there to help flatten her stomach, but Emily had replaced it long ago with the handmade notebook. So far, her mother hadn't found out. She pulled out a silver pencil on a chain around her neck and carefully drew the square imprint.

A trace of a wheel leaves a shadow in the mud.

"He didn't walk here, he drove." She corrected herself. "No, because someone drove the carriage away. He was driven."

"Young lady, what are you doing down there?" A voice from above startled her, and she fell back into the mud.

"Now my back will be as filthy as my front," she grumbled. "Mother will have a fit." She looked up, shading her eyes to block out the afternoon sun. She recognized the portly figure of the constable who split his duties between Amherst and Northampton. "Hello, Constable Chapman."

"Ah, it's Miss Dickinson." He held out a hand and helped her to her feet. "I didn't mean to startle you."

"No harm done," she said. "Thank you."

"What were you doing down there?" he repeated.

Without considering, she said, "I wanted to see how the body came into the pond." His scandalized expression made her wince. When would she learn to think before speaking?

"Miss Dickinson, what would your mother say? Or worse, your father? You should be inside keeping yourself calm, not looking to upset yourself."

She assumed a demure look. "Yes, Constable Chapman. You're right. Are you coming to our house? I'll walk with you."

"I've already been," he said.

Emily knew she had been away for only a few minutes. "Did you talk to Mother?" she asked, eyebrows lifted.

The constable leaned back on his heels and hitched his thumbs under the top of his trousers. "I could see that she wasn't well, so I kept my questions brief."

"What questions?" Emily pressed.

His brow furrowed, but he answered easily enough. "Did you hear anything last night? Did you notice anyone out of the ordinary yesterday? The usual questions I ask in such a situation."

"But they won't get you the answers you need," Emily retorted. "We didn't notice anything because he came into the water over here, out of sight from the house. See the carriage tracks? And then there are footprints going down the bank."

With barely a glance at her evidence, the constable smiled condescendingly. "Then you have solved the mystery. He was probably a tramp who hitched a ride with someone. He got off, slipped down the bank, and then drowned. It's a simple as that—and that's what I'll tell the coroner. There's no need for an inquest."

Emily stared at him. "But we don't know anything yet!" she exclaimed. "We don't even know his name!"

"We will. Someone is bound to know him. I'll inform the town clerk that the death was accidental and I can go back to tracking Mrs. Elmtree's stolen cow." With a polite nod, the constable headed back toward the Common.

"But . . . " Emily watched his retreating back with disgust. "We know nothing, and if you are in charge, we never will." She looked back across the pond, glimpsing her house through the trees.

"I must get a closer look at that body," she said.

Emily waited for what seemed like hours, watching a column of respectable townspeople climb the steps to enter the First Congregational Church of Amherst to view the body. Their puzzled conversations as they left told her that the body was still unidentified. As the time passed, she spared a thought for her mother. She would be livid with Emily for having stayed out so long. But that was nothing to what she would say if she knew where Emily was.

As twilight fell and the good citizens of Amherst retreated to their homes, Emily took her chance. Slipping through the double doors of the church, she went downstairs to the vestry, which was used by the church's congregation and, when needed, by the town. Today it served both masters.

The room was empty except for the body, which lay on a table, covered with a woolen blanket. Several lanterns were placed about the still figure for light, and the smell of burning whale oil hung heavy in the air. As Emily drew closer, her steps grew slower. And slower. She stopped, suddenly reluctant to go any further.

Emily had helped her mother lay out her deceased elderly relatives, and had spent hours sitting with them while they lay in the parlor. Usually she found dead bodies restful; because they had departed this life, they gave her space to think. But those were people she knew, with names and histories. There was no mystery to those bodies. Everything about this corpse was a question. She forced herself to approach.

The dead man's soles faced her. She lifted the blanket just a bit to reveal inexpensive canvas boots. Emily reached out and ran her fingertips over the soles. They were barely scuffed.

"New," she said to herself.

His pants were workman's pants, worn and dirty. They were too short for him; she could see his ankles. She folded back the blanket, noting the dampness, no doubt from the pond. He wore a cotton shirt, like any laborer in town might wear.

This man was a stranger to her, she was sure of it. Finally, just to be certain, she pulled the blanket away from his face.

She stumbled back and fell to the wooden floor.

"Mr. Nobody," she whispered. She swallowed hard to settle her stomach and then rose and approached again, putting her hand to the table to steady herself.

Her hand hovered above his. After a long hesitation, she stroked his left hand. "I'm so sorry," she said. The moist chill of his fingers made her shiver. She remembered the warmth of his skin when he had touched her hand in the stable. She began to weep. No amount of blinking would hold back the tears.

All the while, her mind was racing. Mr. Nobody had been hale and hearty two days earlier. And he had been dressed expensively. Why had he changed his clothes? When she saw him last, he was headed to her father's law office. And the day before that, he had left her to go toward an unpleasant encounter. How had he ended up facedown in the Dickinsons' pond? Was he trying to come to Emily? Might she have saved him if she had only known he was outside?

"Do you know him?" A voice startled her from her reverie. She jumped, and Mr. Nobody's hand flopped to the side of the table. Reverend Colton stood in the doorway.

While she considered her answer, Emily carefully folded Mr. Nobody's hands across his chest. His body was beginning to stiffen, and she had to use more strength than she expected. "I have no idea who he is," she said scrupulously.

The reverend came closer and stared at her. "Have you been crying?"

"Perhaps." Emily sniffed. "It's very sad, isn't it?"

He offered her a handkerchief, which she accepted gratefully. "I never thought of you as sentimental, particularly about someone you've never met." He watched her carefully, as though he doubted her truthfulness.

She hurried to divert his attention. "Did he drown?"

"I assume so. Too many people don't know how to swim; it was probably a tragic accident."

"Even if he knew how to swim, would he go into a pond fully dressed?" she asked doubtfully. And in clothes that weren't his own, she added silently.

"No one has recognized him," he said. "We may never know what happened. Constable Chapman has his work cut out for him."

Emily covered her involuntary snort with a muffled cough. In his mind, Constable Chapman had already closed the case.

"What will happen to him?" she asked.

"In another few days, we'll have to bury him in the potter's field."

The potter's field was the burial ground for strangers and the destitute. "That's terrible," Emily cried. "It would be a sin to bury him without a proper marker."

"Yes, Emily." A pious smile played upon the reverend's lips. "Every soul deserves a proper accounting on earth and in heaven."

"There's power in a name," she said slowly. Her thoughts were racing, but she considered her words carefully before speaking. "Reverend Colton, you said we are all responsible for him."

"Indeed."

"So it's my duty to find out who he was?"

"In a manner of speaking," he said, looking startled. "But I didn't mean you personally."

"But if I can, I must?" Emily was implacable.

Staring down his long nose, he watched her closely. "I think your mother might disapprove."

"She disapproves of many things I want to do," Emily confided.

Reverend Colton considered. "Then perhaps it is better she doesn't find out," he said. "After all, a proper Christian burial is the important thing."

"Yes, yes, of course," Emily breathed, feeling as topsy-turvy as if she were riding a wave of righteousness.

He patted her on the shoulder. "The Lord chooses mysterious vessels to do his will." He pulled out his pocket watch. "I'm due at the Hitchcocks' for dinner. Why don't you precede me, my dear?"

"Reverend, if you don't mind, I'd like to sit here for a moment with this poor man."

He hesitated, then nodded with a gentle smile. "Be sure to lock the door when you leave." He turned and walked away, leaving Emily alone with Mr. Nobody. A draught from the closing door threatened to extinguish the flickering candles.

Emily pulled out her notebook and silver pencil. "Well, then, Mr. Nobody. We have a mission. How can you help me to help you?"

Looking more closely at his shirt, she noticed that the sleeves were far too long for his arms. The material was well-worn but clean. She had already noticed the pants were too short. Gingerly, she pulled at his collar. His head flopped to one side. Murmuring an apology, she peeked to see if there was a label.

The shirt was from Cutler's dry goods store in the center of Amherst. That was surprising. Mr. Nobody was from out of town—why would he shop there? And of course, why would he buy a shirt that was the wrong size and so different from the dapper clothes he seemed to prefer?

She jotted down this first clue: *Clothes alien to himself. Proportions distorted.*

She saw a pale whiteness stuck to the fabric of the collar. Using the tips of her fingers, she pulled out a twisted white flower with a woody stem. She gently separated the petals and held it up to one of the candles illuminating the vestry. The blossom had a ghostly appearance. Emily frowned, trying to recall if she had seen a flower like that near the pond. She didn't think so. She carefully placed it between two pages in the back of her notebook.

As she recalled only too well, Mr. Nobody's hands had been callused. But now she noticed that his nails were trimmed and shaped.

"You pampered yourself when you had the chance," she murmured. "But what's this?" The skin underneath his tidy nails was blue.

Fingernails protect flesh blued with death.

She carefully replaced the blanket over his body and walked upstairs and out into the fresh evening air.

"I could have known his name if I had only asked a second time," she muttered, kicking a stone hard against the wooden church steps. Not one stranger in a thousand would have understood why she wanted a bee to land on her nose. Or would see the humor in her ridiculous parents. Or agree that one could worship God anywhere.

Mr. Nobody had met the real Emily Dickinson, with all her unconventionality, and he had liked her for it. It was up to her to find out his name, and how he came to be floating facedown in her pond.

Drowning is not so pitiful
As the attempt to rise.

CHAPTER 5

The next morning a crow's caw woke Emily. She slid out of bed gingerly, careful not to wake her sister. Vinnie groaned a little and rolled onto her back, her fists flung against the pillow. The day was young, but it looked to be warm. Emily pulled open the window sash and saw a large crow on the path below. Its sleek black feathers ruffled across its back and glistened in the sun.

"How handsome," she whispered. Crows were one of her favorite birds.

With a sharp crack of its ebony beak, the crow viciously split a worm in half, threw it into the air, caught it, and swallowed it in one smooth motion. Emily smiled and tapped on the window. The bird looked up at her with beady eyes. With an angry squawk and flapping of its wings, it flew away toward the graveyard behind the house.

"You're not afraid of anything, are you?" she whispered. "There's a lesson for me in how you get your breakfast. I have to be as fearless as you if I'm to get what I'm after."

Peering over at the bed, Emily reassured herself that Vinnie still slept. Quickly, she pulled out her notebook and scribbled a few lines.

A bird came down the Walk:
He did not know I saw;
He bit an angle-worm in halves
And ate the fellow, raw

Satisfied for the moment, she put away the notebook and made her way downstairs while the rest of the household slept.

Early morning was a favorite time to think, without the press of other minds and idle chatter. Today, with a mysterious death to investigate, she missed her older brother, Austin, who was away at school. Without him, her confidences lacked a receptive ear. Vinnie was willing, but she was younger and too lighthearted. She couldn't be trusted with something as solemn as this.

Emily stoked the stove to boil water for her tea and pondered her next step. Should she start with the beginning or the end? The beginning was her odd meeting with Mr. Nobody four days ago. His death must be the result of something in his life. She had to remember everything he had said. Or she could begin with the ending: The body lying in the church had a tale to tell. Surely both stories would join in the middle. But what to do first?

The kettle whistled, and she poured the steaming water into the pot.

The stairs behind her creaked and Vinnie appeared, wrapped in a thin dressing gown. Not meeting Emily's eye, she said, "I'm going to feed the chickens."

"Say good morning to the kittens for me," Emily said, staring fixedly into the teapot as she measured the loose tea.

A giggle, and Vinnie was out the door.

Once the family was awake, the opportunity for hard thinking was over. Emily turned her attention to the morning's tasks. Their mother planned on preserving tomatoes from the garden. That was to be followed by yet another long afternoon of baking. The weather was already uncomfortably warm. Emily sighed; it was going to be a tedious day.

"Emily, come and see!" Vinnie appeared at the door, her face flushed, eyes dancing. "Mama Tabby is on the hunt!"

Although Emily much preferred birds to cats, Vinnie's enthusiasm was irresistible. Emily followed her sister into the orchard, where the drama was unfolding.

The fat tabby was stalking a huge cardinal that was tugging at a piece of straw for its nest, seemingly oblivious to the impending danger. The cat's stomach brushed the ground as she ran toward her prey, never taking her eyes off its red feathers. All the while she made a stuttering sound in her throat, as though she were already thinking of the juicy morsel the bird would be.

"So help me, Vinnie, if your cat kills that beautiful bird . . ."

With a knowing air, Vinnie interrupted, "The bird isn't in any danger."

Just as Mama Tabby sprang, the cardinal suddenly took flight. The cat sat back on her haunches and started to lick her belly as though nothing had happened.

Emily and Vinnie burst out laughing.

"She never does catch anything!" Vinnie said.

"It's just as well for her kittens that we feed her so well," Emily agreed. "Otherwise they would starve." She glanced about the yard. "Where are they?"

"Down by the water."

"You were at the pond?" Emily asked, surprised.

"I thought it was important the kittens don't get morbid about the pond."

"You mean *you* don't want to become morbid," Emily said.

The sisters looked over to the kittens, who were frolicking where the grass ended in a steep bank at the muddy pond. Suddenly, the largest and boldest one, a black kitten with a white chest, began to slip down the bank. It clawed frantically, but its paws found no purchase in the mud. There was a wicked splash.

Emily and Vinnie rushed to the pond's edge. Vinnie threw herself down on the mud bank to try and reach the cat. "Emily! Help her! She's drowning!" she called frantically.

The kitten thrashed in the water, and Emily could hear its frantic mews. For a moment, she froze.

"Emily!"

Emily's arms weren't long enough to rescue the cat either. She pulled off her slippers and slid into the pond. Spring-fed, the water was always chilled. Her feet sank into the cold muck. The water came to her waist, weighing down her housedress. She tried to move toward the kitten thrashing in the water, but her feet were trapped in the slime.

"Emily, hurry!"

"I *am*," she cried, lifting one foot and then the other. She scooped up the kitten and placed him in Vinnie's waiting hands on shore.

"He's going to die," Vinnie sobbed. Emily couldn't bear the sound of her sister's grief. She pulled herself out of the water, her feet scrabbling against the mud. She slipped, and her heavy skirt dragged her under for a brief moment. She tried to breathe and inhaled water.

For a moment, she let herself float, not trying to rescue herself. The sensation of drowning was new. Her chest began to ache; in spite of herself she struggled to the surface and made her way to the pond's edge.

She spit up water and coughed. Vinnie, still kneeling over the kitten, hadn't even noticed her sister's predicament. More carefully this time, Emily clambered onto shore, grasping at the long grass for support. She lay on the bank, breathing hard, while Vinnie fussed over the tiny cat.

"Emily, he's not breathing!"

"Let me try something," Emily said wearily. She took a corner of Vinnie's dressing gown and wrapped the kitten in it, rubbing it dry. She had once seen a farmer revive a newborn piglet that wasn't breathing by massaging its heart.

Still nothing.

"Emily!"

She rubbed some more. "Wait."

The kitten's thin body convulsed and it coughed, spraying water on Vinnie's dressing gown.

"You saved him!"

After a moment, the kitten mewed and began twisting in Emily's hands to escape. "Ungrateful little beast," Emily laughed. "Next time, be more careful."

Vinnie took the kitten in her arms. "Thank you, Emily." She stared at Emily's sopping white housedress, flapping against her bare legs. "You must go inside and get dry."

Emily walked back to the house, trailing behind her sister. She wrung her long braid free of cold water, reliving the moment when the pond closed over her head. Invading her mind's eye came a vivid image of the dashing Mr. Nobody flailing in the murky pond, his lungs filling with water instead of life-giving air. Unlike with Vinnie's kitten, no one had been there to rescue him. Did he slip quietly into oblivion or did he call for help? Why didn't the Dickinsons hear him?

Her ruminations were interrupted by the familiar sight of Dr. Gridley coming down the road, just outside their garden. Every day, while she prepared breakfast, she saw him setting off toward the fields north of town. It was like a secret meeting between them, although they never spoke.

But today she would alter that comfortable pattern. The doctor was certain to have the answers she needed. Despite her sodden skirts, she rushed out to the gate and hailed him.

Surprised, Dr. Gridley's long stride faltered. "Hello, Miss Dickinson."

She moved to the fence between them. "Dr. Gridley," she began without ceremony. "You examined the stranger we found in the pond."

Taken aback, he nodded. His expression grew even more puzzled when he saw Emily's wet condition. "Miss Emily, are you well?"

"I am perfectly well," Emily said, trying to hide her impatience. "Just tell me, did he drown?"

"I assume he drowned. He was found in your pond, after all." He stared at her, speculation in his eyes. "Did you fall in yourself?"

Emily ignored his question. "Are you certain that he drowned?"

"I'd have to examine his lungs . . . "

"To see whether there is water in them?" she finished, remembering how the kitten had coughed up pond water. As had she.

"Well, yes." His forehead gleamed with a sheen of perspiration.

Emily thought for a moment. "Tell me, would his fingernails turn blue if he had drowned?"

Dr. Gridley's eyes widened. "A peculiar question to hear on a country lane before breakfast."

MICHAELA MACCOLL

"I noticed his fingernails had a bluish tinge, like an iris." She made her observation almost a question.

"You saw the body?" he asked, incredulous.

"Of course," Emily said. "He was found on my family's property. My father is worried that he might be a client. He wants me to gather all the information I can." She felt guilty misrepresenting her father, but it was a necessary lie if she were to enlist Dr. Gridley's help. "So, the fingernails?"

"I don't normally associate blueness with drowning . . . but, really, he was found in a pond! Of course he drowned. You can tell your father that I've already informed Constable Chapman of the cause of death."

"Dr. Gridley." She reached over and touched his hand. "My father wouldn't want you to take anything for granted."

Almost as if against his will, he said slowly, "I could examine him again. I may see more today."

"The dead can change?" Emily asked dubiously.

"Sometimes I'll see bruises the next day that aren't apparent immediately after death."

"Like a flower that blooms at night to startle you in the morning?" Emily suggested.

Dr. Gridley waggled his finger at her. "An original mind, indeed, Emily Dickinson."

Emily shrugged off the compliment, if a compliment it was, and asked simply, "Will you help me?"

He tugged on the point of his white beard. "I'll look at the body again."

"And check his lungs for water," she reminded him.

He nodded. "But if I find anything, I have to let the authorities know."

"Of course. Thank you, Dr. Gridley." She tucked a long, wet strand of hair behind her ear. "It would ease my mind."

But she knew that until she discovered who Mr. Nobody was and how he had died, her mind would never be at ease.

I shall forget the drop of anguish

That scalds me now, that scalds me now.

CHAPTER 6

Emily's investigation was well begun with her conversation with Dr. Gridley. What next? If she returned to the kitchen, Vinnie would never let her leave. She swerved to the little-used front door. Opening it just wide enough to slip in, Emily stole upstairs to get out of her wet dress and shoes. She scowled at the pile of wet laundry accumulating in the basket. Laundry day would come around again much too soon. As if she weren't in enough trouble with her mother already.

A few minutes later, changed into a walking dress and her damp hair pinned up respectably, Emily ran silently down the front stairs. As she turned the corner, she came face to face with Vinnie carrying a tray of tea.

"Watch out!" Vinnie cried. The tea sloshed out of the cup onto the tray. Vinnie gave her sister a dark look. "Where have you been? I've had to make Mama's tea myself."

Emily hurried to explain before Vinnie could begin reciting her litany of grievances. "I was outside with Dr. Gridley. And then I had to change my dress. I was all wet after I saved your kitten," she said pointedly.

"I already thanked you," Vinnie said. "Mother isn't feeling well again. I think we'll have to do the tomatoes tomorrow."

"Excellent," Emily said. "I have better things to do."

"You're thinking about that body again, aren't you?" Vinnie accused. "I know where you were yesterday. Don't deny it. If Mother knew, she would have a fit."

"Then we mustn't tell her," Emily said earnestly. "For her health's sake."

"You mean so you can be free to do whatever you like."

Shrugging, Emily squashed her bonnet over her hair.

"Where are you going?" Vinnie's voice rose in pitch. "I'm not baking by myself today."

"We need sugar. I'll get some from the store." Emily stepped toward the front door.

"Emily Elizabeth, don't you dare abandon me again!" Vinnie cried. "We have plenty of sugar."

"Then salt." Emily flung open the door.

"We have a whole box. Emily, come back at once!"

Before Vinnie finished her sentence, Emily was through the garden gate and up the hill to Cutler's dry goods store.

Amherst had two general stores. Mr. Nobody's new clothes had come from Cutler's. Unfortunately, the Dickinson family patronized a rival store, Mack and Sons. Emily had rarely shopped at Cutler's, whose owner had a crotchety reputation.

Mr. Cutler himself was behind the counter, his skeletal body framed by shelves that stretched to the ceiling. He was waiting on a little boy who was fetching baking powder for his mother. Emily could see the boy eyeing the jars of candy on the counter.

As she waited, Emily looked around the store. In the far corner was a table stacked with work shirts and pants. She felt the fabric of a rough blue shirt and examined the label inside the collar. It was identical to Mr. Nobody's. The trousers, too, were familiar. The canvas boots she was looking for were in neat rows on the shelves against the wall.

"That will be two pennies, son," Mr. Cutler said from behind the counter.

The boy stuck out a palm containing exactly two pennies. He glanced again at the jars, his gaze lingering first on the butterscotch, then the caramels and the peppermints before coming to rest on the lollipops.

"Thank you," the boy muttered. He took his little package of baking powder and shuffled out.

Emily stepped up and put a penny on the counter. "May I have a lollipop? Quickly, please."

Deft from long practice, the dour storekeeper folded up the candy in a twist of paper.

"I'll just be a moment." Emily hurried out and saw the little boy had gone no further than the wide porch outside. "Here you are," she said, handing him the candy. Without stopping for the boy's thanks, she returned to the store counter, a smile on her lips.

Mr. Cutler's face was still grim. "What do you need today, Miss Dickinson?"

Emily sighed. Did everyone in town know who she was? "Mr. Cutler, I'd like to ask you something rather unusual."

He waited.

"Have you sold one of those shirts and a pair of pants together? Perhaps the boots as well?"

With a bark of laughter, Mr. Cutler said, "Do you know how many of these I sell? Every farmhand and factory worker in Amherst wears my clothes."

Emily refused to be discouraged. "Would you recall if a gentleman had purchased such a combination?"

"And if I did, why should I tell you? My customers rely on my discretion."

"For the purchase of work clothing?"

"For any purchase. Tell me young lady, why are you ask-ing?" He paused, but Emily couldn't think of a reasonable answer. "Do you want to buy anything?" he asked point-edly. "Another candy, perhaps?"

She decided to abandon the clothes for now. She had one more clue to follow. "Honey," she said.

"How much?" Mr. Cutler appeared to soften a bit, like a dollop of honey melting into hot tea, Emily thought whimsically.

"I'm looking for a particular type," she said. "It's an unusual flavor—with apple, clover, and a hint of honeysuckle."

"Fancy." Mr. Cutler scowled. "I don't have any more."

"But you did at one time?"

He nodded. "Not now. I can offer you a honey that tastes of wildflowers."

"I want only this particular honey," Emily insisted.

"My honey isn't good enough for you?"

Flustered, Emily sought the words to soothe the can-tankerous shopkeeper. "I'm sure your honey is delicious, but my mother is partial to the honeysuckle."

"I never have much to sell. Sam Wentworth only sells enough to pay for his groceries. And none at all this year."

"Sam Wentworth?" Emily pounced. "I don't know him. Where does he live?"

"You don't want to drop in on him. He doesn't like peo-ple much." Mr. Cutler sounded as if he was in complete sympathy. Emily wondered why he kept a shop if he disliked the public so.

"I'm sure when I compliment his honey, he won't mind," Emily said.

"Find him yourself. It's not my job to send customers elsewhere."

"It was a civil request . . . " Emily began.

"Civil?" Mr. Cutler snorted. "You Dickinsons had your noses in the air and your heads in the clouds. My store has been too good for you all these years, but now you ask me your impertinent questions. And to add insult to injury, you want me to help you buy honey somewhere else. Cutler's doesn't need your business, Miss Dickinson."

Emily was unused to discourtesy in any form. Usually the name Dickinson opened every door in town. "Thank you for your time, Mr. Cutler. I'll be certain to tell my father of your courtesy." She turned on her heel and stalked away from the counter. She bumped into someone standing in the doorway.

"Miss Emily?" It was her father's law clerk, Mr. Ripley.

"Mr. Ripley." Emily worked to keep surprise out of her voice. Although her father's office was on the street adjoining the Common, she rarely saw Mr. Ripley outside of it. "You're playing truant from the office?" she asked.

He began to rub his hands together nervously. "I needed tea," he said. Everything about him was nondescript. His height was middling and his mousy brown hair was parted on one side, giving him a lopsided look. Emily usually had the impression Mr. Ripley did not expect to be noticed. Today he seemed anxious.

Before Emily could make her way past him, he asked, "Did I hear you mention Mr. Wentworth?"

She blushed as she realized that Mr. Ripley had no doubt overheard Mr. Cutler's rudeness. "Yes. Mr. Sam Wentworth seems to be responsible for some exceptional honey. Do you know where he lives?"

"Oh, that Mr. Wentworth." His face went slack. "I think he lives on the road to Northampton. I don't know. If you'll excuse me, I must go." Without lingering to make his purchases, he scurried back toward the law offices of Edward Dickinson.

"But your tea!" Emily called after him. Mr. Ripley didn't stop, and Emily stared after him, perplexed.

The grubby little boy was still sitting on the porch steps, sucking hard on the lollipop. His earnestness made her smile. He pulled the boiled taffy out of his mouth and said, "That man was wrong. Mr. Wentworth lives out toward Pelham. It's a red house, on the right side of the road, but you can hardly see for the apple orchard. The house needs paint."

Before she could thank the boy, he had popped the lollipop back in his mouth and shuffled away.

This Mr. Wentworth sold—or gave—Mr. Nobody a bit of fresh honeycomb a few days earlier, Emily thought. Surely he must know the man's identity. And if Emily were lucky, perhaps Mr. Wentworth knew more than that. But would he tell her?

The pedigree of honey
Does not concern the bee—
A clover, any time, to him
Is aristocracy.

CHAPTER 7

Emily marched purposefully down Main Street in the direction of Pelham. Silhouetted against the sky, a crow perched on the roof of a large house, its sharp eyes watching her. As she passed the house, it screeched. Its cawing was answered by a chorus of other crows in the elm trees scattered around the garden.

Emily stopped to stare and savor the moment. "'The ancient crows hold their sour conversation in the sky,'" she recited aloud. Ralph Waldo Emerson had a way with a poem. Her father didn't approve of her reading modern poetry, but she secretly considered Mr. Emerson a kindred spirit. When she read his poetry, she felt as though she were flying.

She continued past farms and meadows. Emily's doubts about the wisdom of her excursion increased with every step away from her familiar neighborhood. After a mile or so, she spied her goal. The property was impossible to mistake, with its overgrown apple orchard and enormous honeysuckle bushes competing for air and light. Through the tangled branches, she glimpsed a tiny red house with peeling paint. The porch railing had rotted through and had fallen into jagged pieces on the porch. The shutters hung crookedly, and one dangled by a single rusted nail.

She hesitated, her hand on the gate. Across the road was a field of corn, the tall stalks swaying in the faint breeze. A scarecrow in the center of the field seemed to question her resolve. Emily looked down the road in both directions. It was reasonably busy with passing carriages and wagons. At least she wasn't completely alone.

She pushed open a creaking gate and stepped carefully through the brambles. They grabbed at her ankles as though they were trying to snare her. She steeled herself to keep going.

Although there was no sign of human activity, everywhere there was movement. Bees darted among the apple blossoms, the honeysuckle, the clover. Emily hesitated, staring up at the forbidding house. She wasn't one to shirk her self-imposed duty, but she was reluctant to climb those rickety steps and knock on that door.

But perhaps she didn't have to. The honey had led her here. If the honey was not the same, she need not knock. It was only prudent to verify the flavors first, she thought. She pushed away the knowledge that she was being cowardly.

Through the trees, she saw half a dozen wooden hives. She went closer. Glancing back, she was relieved to see that the house was lost to view behind a dozen apple trees. She wouldn't be observed.

Each box quivered with the crawling of hundreds—no, thousands—of bees. The thrum of their activity made the bones behind her ears shiver. Her brother had tried to keep bees one summer without success, so she had some experience with the creatures.

Trying to act as though she had every right to do so, she lifted the top of a hive and peered inside. She could see the honey in combs at the bottom, their sweetness out of reach.

Emily climbed on an old crate and reached down to the honeycomb. In an instant, her hand was carpeted with swarming insects. The bees whirred, and she felt as though she were buzzing too. She didn't dare move and for a moment the honey was forgotten, as was her investigation. Emily couldn't take her eyes off her hand, as though it were something separate from herself. She had never felt anything as consuming as the sensation of a thousand bees crawling across her skin.

A bee flew up and tangled itself in her hair. With her free hand, Emily shooed it away and brought herself back to her task. Gently brushing the bees off her hand, she broke off a piece of comb, soaked with honey the color of burnt gold.

Carefully replacing the hive's cover, she moved away and brought the honeycomb to her lips. It dripped in her hand, staining her sleeve. It smelled like perfume distilled from the orchard and flowers all around her. Her finger touched her lips and the burst of flavor spread through her limbs.

It was unmistakably the same honey. Mr. Nobody had been here. He had tasted this honey and carried some away to Emily. She floated on the memory of his callused finger on the tip of her nose.

"Ow!" While Emily was lost in her reverie, a furious bee that had followed her from the hive stung her hand. She dropped the honeycomb and took stock of the damage. A stinger was sticking upright in her skin. Wincing, she pulled it out. She prodded at the small swollen lump, acutely aware of the poison spreading through her blood like the bindweed that infiltrated her flowerbeds.

Emily looked around for the well that she knew must be there—cold water would relieve the sting. Unfortunately, wells were always close to houses. Now that she knew that Mr. Wentworth's honey was the same as Mr. Nobody's, she would have to approach anyway. She made her way through the orchard toward the dilapidated house.

As she trudged forward, she heard faint voices from inside the house. She abandoned the idea of finding the well and wondered whether she should knock on the door—or would she learn more if she played spy?

Straining to hear the voices, she approached as stealthily as one of Vinnie's hunting cats. Emily detoured from the front door to a window, open to catch the least breeze. She flattened her body below the sill and listened hard. The heat felt as though it was pressing down on her skin. Her heart hammered in her ears, nearly drowning out the voices of the men inside.

"If you love your family, Henry, go back to New Haven. Please." It was an old man's voice, full of strain. He must be Mr. Wentworth, Emily thought, wiping perspiration from her forehead.

"Not until I have some answers," a younger male voice replied. "Uncle, did you know my cousin . . . ?"

"What do you know about him?" the old man asked warily.

"He's alive—that's the most surprising thing." His voice was bitter. Emily raised her eyebrows.

"Henry, go back to school. We don't need you here." The old man's voice had equal parts anger and fear.

Emily felt breathless with her success. Mr. Nobody had been here—this was established by the honey. Mr. Nobody had told her he had come to town on family business, and here was this Henry, surprised to see his cousin. Was Mr. Nobody his cousin? But then why would Henry be surprised he was alive? She pressed her body close to the wall and felt the splintered wood against her cheek.

"What were you thinking?" Henry asked angrily. "Didn't you realize it was a fraud? Mother could go to jail!"

"Don't judge her. After all, she did it so you could go back to school."

"Jail?" Emily nearly spoke aloud. Mr. Nobody had mentioned a crime. She hoisted herself closer, pulling herself up on the windowsill. But the sill, as dilapidated as the rest of the house, disintegrated in her hands with a loud crack.

She dropped to the ground and huddled against the wall, praying that no one had heard the noise. Her legs trembled, begging her to run, but surely that would draw even more attention. She closed her eyes and made herself feel small. After a few moments that felt like hours, she decided that she was safe.

An angry voice drove every thought of safety from her mind. "What are you doing here?"

Emily's eyes flew open and her breath was shallow. A furious old man with a red face, standing not three feet from her dusty boots, stared down at her.

"Mr. Wentworth?" she asked, her voice trembling.

"Who is asking?" A white crown of hair gave him an aspect of a snowy owl. His white bushy eyebrows punctuated pale blue eyes that raked her from head to toe. He saw the honey on her dress and his eyes grew even more hostile. "You stole my honey!"

Emily clambered to her feet and arranged her skirt. After a steadying breath, she replied, "I wasn't stealing. I was comparing your honey with some I tasted four days ago. It was the same."

"You're mistaken. I didn't even sell any to that thief Cutler this year. No one has my honey but me. Get out." He gestured to the gate.

"A young man gave me the honey," she insisted, resisting the almost overwhelming desire to bolt for home. There were facts here to be discovered.

Mr. Nobody had said he had a relative who raised bees. Emily stared at Mr. Wentworth, comparing his features with her memory of Mr. Nobody's. Was there a resemblance? If Mr. Nobody had had the chance to grow old, would his blond hair have turned white? She couldn't be sure.

"I'm not interested in your nonsense." Mr. Wentworth turned to go back in the house, walking with a slight limp. Without looking back, he said, "My bees don't like visitors and neither do I."

A young man appeared from around the corner of the house. Emily caught her breath. The irrational hope that flared in her breast was followed by a stab of disappointment. The newcomer might have the same build as Mr. Nobody and possess the same voice, but he was a stranger. And of course, the greatest difference of all: This young man was alive.

"Uncle, there's no one around back." He saw Emily and stopped short. "Who is this?"

"She's leaving," Mr. Wentworth said, pausing on the first step of the rickety porch.

Emily summoned her courage. "Mr. Wentworth, to whom did you give a chunk of honeycomb on Friday? Honeycomb that tasted of clover, honeysuckle, and apples?"

He came back and stood close—too close—to Emily, staring suspiciously. She held her ground with an effort; she had never seen a man so tightly wound around his own temper.

"I was in Northampton, buying a new carriage," he answered grudgingly. "Not that it's any of your business."

Emily turned to the nephew, steeling herself to look him in the face. "What about you, then?" she asked, remembering not to betray her eavesdropping by calling him Henry. "Perhaps a long-lost member of the family came to visit and you offered him some honey?"

The young man's face darkened and he burst out, "I don't talk about my family to strangers."

"I told you that someone was listening outside the window," Mr. Wentworth said grimly. He moved closer to Emily. The nephew shifted from one foot to another and licked his lips nervously. Emily felt her breath come more quickly. She retreated and found herself backed against the house. Mr. Wentworth came toward her.

Suddenly there were voices from the road. Through the apple trees, Emily saw a farmer and a lad driving a small herd of cows toward town.

"Uncle . . . " the young man said urgently.

Emily seized her chance. While their attention was on the potential witnesses, she gathered all her fear and courage and took off through the trees. She was halfway to the road before Mr. Wentworth even saw that she was gone.

Bursting though the creaking gate, she startled the farmer and his cows. Falling into step with her unlikely rescuers, she glanced back. Mr. Wentworth had taken a few steps, but his nephew restrained him. Their glares followed her down the dirt road.

Nature—the gentlest mother is.

Impatient of no child—

The feeblest or the waywardest—

Her admonition mild—

CHAPTER 8

It was afternoon by the time Emily arrived home; she had missed dinner. She went straight to the pump in the garden. Her skin was tight with dried sweat. Cupping her hands to catch the ice-cold water, she splashed her face. Then she filled the tin cup hanging on a hook by the pump and drank until she was as refreshed as she could be without a change of clothing.

Eyeing the house, she decided to enter by the front door. With any luck, her mother would still be resting and Emily could slip by and postpone the inevitable scolding. Since Emily knew exactly what would be said, she saw no reason to rush toward the confrontation.

"Emily Elizabeth!"

Perhaps there was no more luck to be had today.

"Where have you been?" Her mother was waiting in the parlor. She must have been watching for Emily's return. "Look at that dress! You'll be lucky if those stains come out. What have you been doing to get so dirty?"

Emily felt fatigued down to the marrow of her bones. Her feet hurt and the bee sting throbbed. Worse, her chest was beginning to feel hollow, a sure sign that the coughing was not too far behind. Once her mother heard her cough, Emily's freedom would be gone. She needed to rest and, above all, she needed time to think. But her mother's anger filled the room.

"Well, Emily?"

"Mother, I'm confused. Which question should I answer first?" She felt guilty the moment she said it. It was one of her worst character flaws to resort to impertinence when she was in the wrong.

"Emily, your tone is unacceptable." Her mother pushed herself up from the chair. Emily could make out the spidery veins under the surface of her mother's pale complexion. With a rush of contrition, she hurried to her mother's side and placed a careful arm around her waist.

"Mother, you don't look well. Let me help you to bed." She led her mother upstairs to her bedroom, a room that felt too large when Mr. Dickinson was away.

"Emily . . ."

"Mother, I know I've been an awful daughter. Please don't exhaust yourself by scolding me right now." Emily added mischievously, "If you like, I can punish myself while you take a nap."

In spite of herself, a wan smile appeared on her mother's lips.

"I'll be better, I promise." Emily fluffed her mother's pillow and tucked a quilt around her mother's legs.

"You will have no choice," Mrs. Dickinson said simply. "Your father is coming home."

Emily's hands froze. "Father?"

Mrs. Dickinson closed her eyes and said sleepily, "Yes. I asked him to come home for a quick visit. If you won't pay me any attention, I know you'll listen to him."

"When will he be here?"

"Next Monday."

That meant Emily had only six days to discover the identity of Mr. Nobody and why he died. Not a long time, especially when she had chores. But Mr. Dickinson worried about Emily's health, too. He could not be got around as easily as her mother. And with a sinking stomach, Emily realized that once Mr. Dickinson found out what she was doing, her investigation would be over.

She drew the curtains in her mother's room and was closing the door quietly behind her when her mother's voice, still gentle but with a hint of steel, said, "Emily, my dear, tomorrow you'll do the laundry by yourself."

All solicitude for her invalid mother forgotten, Emily protested loudly, "By myself! That will take an eternity. It's not fair."

"Your sister isn't jumping into ponds or rolling in the grass. Your soiled dresses make up half the laundry basket. You *will* do it by yourself."

"Yes, Mother," Emily said dutifully, though she was seething. How could she pursue her investigations while she was up to her elbows in soapy water? But there was no arguing with her mother once her mind was made up.

"Emily, sometimes I think you don't listen to my stories from the newspaper. Do you remember the girl in Atlanta who died of overexertion? She was running outside." Her mother was still mumbling drowsily as Emily closed the door. "I daresay her dress was dirty, too."

Fifteen minutes later, Emily was in a clean dress and her hair was neatly brushed and securely tucked under a net cap. She went warily down the back stairs to the kitchen. The encounter with her mother had gone so poorly that she could not predict how sour Vinnie's welcome would be. But when she came into the kitchen there were no remonstrations, no temper—not even a question. Vinnie was finishing up the washing from the dinner that Emily had missed.

"Vinnie?" There was no reply. "Darling Vinnie, I'm so sorry."

Silence.

"I had something important to do and I lost track of time. Please forgive me."

Vinnie finished the last dish. She dried her hands and calmly walked past Emily into the parlor. Emily, growing frustrated, followed. "Vinnie, I said I was sorry. You're being petty."

As Emily had hoped, Vinnie couldn't stand to be put in the wrong. She whirled around and faced her sister, hands on her hips. "Petty? I did your chores today. I told tales to keep you out of trouble. I prepared dinner by myself. And I took care of mother. I haven't had a moment to myself all day!"

Emily clasped her sister's hands between her own. "I know, darling Vinnie. And it's my fault. Tomorrow you shall gambol with your kittens and eat bonbons all day if I have to make them myself." With an air of extreme virtue, she said, "I'll even do all the laundry alone."

"You are a complete fraud." Vinnie burst out laughing.

"I know that Mother is making you do the washing tomorrow, so don't offer it up to me on a sacrificial platter!"

"All right, I'll clean the chamber pots for a week!"

"Now that is a sacrifice." Vinnie grinned.

Relieved to have her sister's good humor back, Emily sank onto the sofa.

"If you were truly sorry," Vinnie said as she perched in the coziest armchair, "you would tell me what you've been doing."

Emily hesitated. "I can't."

"Why not?" Vinnie gave her a sly look. "It's not as if I haven't already guessed."

A succession of images flashed through Emily's mind. Mr. Nobody in the meadow. His catching her unawares at the smithy's stable. His lifeless body laid out in the cold vestry.

"Whatever do you mean?" she asked in a small voice.

"At first I thought it was about that awful body. But you were mysterious even before that. I thought and thought and then I realized the truth. You have a beau! It's the only explanation. As I've been doing all your chores, I've been wracking my mind trying to decide who it is. Most of the College boys are gone for the break. No one in town has interested you before. Before I die of curiosity, who is it?"

"Nobody." Emily stood up abruptly and walked out of the room.

Tell him night finished before we finished

CHAPTER 9

"Emily, what are you scribbling in your little book?" Vinnie asked as she climbed into their bed.

"Never you mind," Emily said from the window seat. It was just getting dark outside; soon the church bells would ring to warn all respectable citizens to be inside and ready for bed. This was often Emily's only time to write in peace, even if she had to do it by candlelight. What would her family think if they saw the list of clues filling the pages of her precious notebook?

Uncle and Nephew—bound together by blood and secrets.

She had puzzled for hours over what had happened at the farmhouse. She couldn't discount her one piece of solid evidence: Mr. Nobody had been carrying a fresh piece of honeycomb that he must have gotten at the farm. And Sam Wentworth's behavior was undoubtedly suspicious.

Honey, shimmering with the taste of summer, sweeter than the irascible beekeeper.

Perhaps Henry, Mr. Wentworth's nephew, had given the honeycomb to Mr. Nobody. His behavior and the words she had overheard were intriguing.

Another odd detail involved her father's law clerk, Mr. Ripley. When he had heard the name Wentworth, he had behaved very strangely. And of course, she couldn't forget that Mr. Nobody had asked her the way to the law offices of Edward Dickinson.

What connection did Mr. Nobody have with the Wentworths and her father's office? Mr. Ripley wouldn't tell her; she would have to discover it for herself. Luckily, she knew where her father kept the spare key to his office. All she had to do was wait until the household was quiet.

She snuffed out her candle and slipped into the bed next to Vinnie, who was already half asleep. Lying motionless, Emily listened to Vinnie's deep regular breathing. When the darkness seemed thick enough to conceal her, she slid out of bed. She had placed a simple dress at hand, ready to pull on.

She picked up her boots and quietly let herself out of the room. The grandfather clock chimed midnight as she slipped down the stairs.

Emily went to her father's desk and took his spare keys. Gusts of wind rattled the window.

The wind—tapped like a tired Man—.

Emily stopped and lit a candle. She pulled out her notebook and jotted down her thought—she wanted to think about that line some more.

A few minutes later, she was walking rapidly up the hill toward the Common, swinging a covered oil lamp. The hairs on the back of her neck prickled, and she glanced over her shoulder. There was no one there. Not for the first time, Emily noticed that the knowledge that you were misbehaving played tricks on your mind.

She was surprised to see the windows of the Amherst House Hotel were brightly lit, and the noise of men laughing and talking spilled out onto the Common. From the sound of it, the tavern was doing a fine business on a Tuesday night.

Edward Dickinson's law office was on the second floor of a brick building on the street adjacent to the hotel. Keeping to the shadows, she was grateful that the town had not yet lit the Common with gaslights. The darkness preserved her reputation. She cringed to think of her father's reaction if he knew what she was doing. All the more reason to do it now before he came home.

Looking around carefully, Emily dug in her skirt pocket for the heavy iron key and opened the door. One last glance around to be sure she wasn't seen, and she was inside the vestibule and climbing the stairs.

Emily unlocked the door and held the unshielded lantern high to take a good look at the main room. It was familiar to her, but in the dark it took on an eerie air.

Her father had a private office, but Mr. Ripley's desk was out here, as were the files. Last summer when Mr. Ripley had been ill, Emily had helped her father with the filing for a month. She knew her father's byzantine system backward and forward. Armed with the name "Wentworth," she was sure she could find what she needed.

On the right were files related to litigation: cases that would go to court, both criminal and civil. Mr. Nobody had spoken of accounts that needed settling—perhaps he meant before a judge? She started there, with the Ws. Nothing.

On the far wall was a cabinet in which wills were kept. These, she thought, had possibilities. Her persistence was rewarded with a thin folder marked Wentworth.

She brought it to Mr. Ripley's desk and positioned the lamp so she could read. Her fingertips hovered above the folder—what would her father think of her looking at confidential files? She was invading Mr. Wentworth's privacy in a herself would find intolerable. Then she recalled the honey on her nose, and she opened the file.

The will didn't belong to the beekeeper, Samuel Wentworth, at all. It was the last will and testament of another man: Jeremiah Wentworth, Deceased. She checked his date of birth; he had been an old man when he died. She remembered Mr. Nobody's handkerchief marked "JW"— was there a link between him and Jeremiah, Deceased?

The will was dated seven years earlier and had been drafted by her father—she recognized his copperplate printing. The will was brief: If Jeremiah should die, he left small bequests to his brother, Sam, and to his sister, Violet Langston.

Sam Wentworth was the beekeeper. "Violet Langston," Emily murmured. "Who lives on College Street, here in town." She smiled to herself; Violet's name opened up a new avenue of investigation.

The bulk of Jeremiah's estate went to his son, James. There was a list of properties and investments that made Emily raise her eyebrows. Jeremiah had been a very rich man. According to his death certificate, he had died the previous Christmas.

The next page in the file was a codicil. Emily smiled, remembering how she had once asked her father what a "codicil" was—she had loved the round sound of the word. He had explained it was a document added to a will after

MICHAELA MACCOLL

it was written. She frowned; she knew it should always be attached to the will, not lying loose in the file.

This codicil was written in Mr. Ripley's hand, which was not nearly as elegant as her father's. It amended the will to eliminate James as the primary heir because he had died before his father. It was dated the previous November, just after Thanksgiving.

Without James to inherit, the money went to Jeremiah's brother, Sam, and his sister, Violet. Emily wondered why Sam's house was so dilapidated if he had inherited half of a huge fortune.

She rifled through the remaining papers and found only some correspondence and a copy of the application to have the will probated. She knew her father was conscientious to a fault—so where was the death certificate for the son, James?

"Who's here?" The door slammed open. A voice from the doorway was like a clap of thunder. Emily closed the file and shoved it back in the drawer.

"I have a shotgun! I'll shoot!" The voice wasn't quite as bold as the words, but Emily thought she recognized it. She hastily lifted the lantern to show her face. "Mr. Ripley, is that you?" she asked. The light quivered in her trembling hand.

"Miss Emily?" Mr. Ripley stepped into the office, still aiming the shotgun in her direction. "What are you doing here?"

"I can explain," Emily said. She backed away and moved behind his desk. She opened her mouth, but her usual facile explanations deserted her. How could she possibly explain her presence?

"What are you doing here?" he repeated, coming close enough so that she could smell whiskey on his breath.

"Perhaps you might put the weapon away," Emily said. She kept her eyes on the shotgun until Mr. Ripley, looking slightly shamefaced, broke open the barrel and laid the gun safely on the table. "Thank you."

A thought occurred to her. "Where did that gun come from?"

"I keep this locked in the outside closet," he said. "But why are you here?"

With a sinking stomach, she realized that Mr. Ripley was bound to tell her father everything. Her only option was to take the offensive. "What are you doing out so late at night? My father prefers his clerks to be sober. I'm sure he would not approve of you carousing."

Mr. Ripley took a step backward. "Miss Emily, I assure you my habits are regular indeed. Tonight I was celebrating a special occasion. . . . I am engaged to be married."

"Congratulations, Mr. Ripley," Emily said. "Who is the fortunate lady?"

But the clerk would not be deflected. "I must insist you tell me why you are here. Has Mr. Dickinson returned?" He glanced toward his employer's dark office.

A third voice startled both of them. "I can explain." Emily and Mr. Ripley turned with astonishment to the doorway to see Vinnie. She was wrapped in her mother's shawl and clutching a lantern.

"Miss Lavinia!"

"Vinnie, what are you doing here?"

Vinnie hurried over to Emily and embraced her. "It's all right now, dear sister. I'm here to bring you home." She turned to Mr. Ripley and spoke in a confidential voice, as though Emily were not in the room at all. "She has these turns."

Emily stiffened, but her sister squeezed her shoulders in warning.

"Turns?" Mr. Ripley repeated.

"She gets obsessed. Last year it was my mother's recipes. Emily could be found at all hours sorting through them—to no purpose, mind you—just for the sake of touching each one, over and over again. Tonight she began talking about Father's papers in just the same way."

Mortified, Emily stared down at Mr. Ripley's desk. Her attention was distracted from Vinnie's nonsense by the blotting pad. She could make out the word Wentworth, reversed on the blotting paper, but legible nonetheless. What had Mr. Ripley been writing recently that involved the Wentworths?

Vinnie was still prattling. "When I saw that she had Father's keys, I suspected she might come here—so I followed her." She gestured to her cloth shoes, so much less suitable for walking than Emily's sensible boots. "But she walks much faster than I."

"I had no idea," Mr. Ripley said. "Although now that I think on it, she often says very odd things."

Emily straightened and was about to speak her mind when she was forestalled by Vinnie.

"I'm sure you can appreciate that we like to keep Emily's little problem within the family circle. Can I depend on you not to mention this? Not even to Father—he worries so."

"Of course, of course," Mr. Ripley said. "You may count on my discretion."

"Thank you!" Vinnie beamed.

"Would you like me to help you bring her home?" Mr. Ripley asked.

Vinnie shook her head. "Now that the mania has left her, I'll have no trouble with her."

Emily glared at her sister, but Vinnie ignored her.

"I'll lock up for you," Mr. Ripley said.

"And I'll return Father's key to its rightful place. Mr. Ripley, I can't thank you enough." While Vinnie was talking, Emily stealthily stuffed the blotting paper in her pocket.

"Good night, Misses Dickinson."

Emily let Vinnie lead her quickly out of the office, down

the stairs, and past the Common. "Vinnie!" she panted, trying to catch her breath. "I can't believe you said those things. Next you'll have me committed to an asylum."

Vinnie stopped in the middle of North Pleasant Street, now illuminated by a thin crescent of moon and brilliant stars. "Emily, what did you want me to say? He caught you snooping in Father's papers." She lifted her thick braid of hair to cool her face and neck. "I thought I was quite clever. He feels as though we've confided in him—and you know how virtuous he is. He'll never tell anyone."

"He might tell his fiancée," Emily pointed out, unwilling to give Vinnie the satisfaction of having rescued her.

"Fiancée?" Vinnie was easily diverted. "How can Mr. Ripley afford to get married? Father always said he was poor as a church mouse."

"Perhaps he came into money recently?" Emily dangled the question in front of Vinnie like an apple in front of their horse, Jasper.

Vinnie shook her head violently. "Emily, you are doing it again. Trying to distract me. What does it matter if Mr. Ripley is getting married? What were you really doing in Father's office?"

"I take these turns . . . sometimes I can't help myself," Emily replied in an arch voice.

"This is the final straw, Emily Elizabeth Dickinson." Vinnie stamped her foot on the dirt road. "I've put up with your morbid fascination with that dead man. I covered for your truancy when you should be sharing our chores, and I rescued you from your own foolishness just now. It was all fine and well when I thought you were in love, but that doesn't seem to be the case." A disappointed expression flitted across her face. "If you don't tell me everything, and I mean everything, I'm informing Mother about where I found you tonight."

"But she'll tell Father."

Vinnie nodded with a sly smile.

There was a silence between the sisters. Finally Vinnie said, "So? Will you tell me or not?"

Until now, Emily's investigation had been hers alone, a private thing between her and the shade of Mr. Nobody. But now she suspected fraud, and possibly murder. And the corruption might have spread to her own father's office. Maybe it was no coincidence that Mr. Nobody had been found in their pond. Might Vinnie have the right to know? Perhaps she could help.

"It's a long story," Emily warned.

"We have all night."

Emily couldn't help feeling relieved. It would be a burden shared. "All right," she said. "I'll tell you."

"Everything?"

"Everything."

One Sister have I in our house.

CHAPTER 10

Emily poked the fire banked in the stove until she had enough flame to light a candle. Taking a pitcher from the icebox, she poured two glasses of milk, partnering them with generous slices of gingerbread. She thought for a few moments, trying to arrange her story.

Vinnie suddenly interrupted her musing. "When Austin is home, you and he are down here talking after we're all in bed, aren't you?" Vinnie's normally cheerful voice held a touch of bitterness.

Emily raised her eyebrows. "Sometimes. We began the habit years ago—you were too young to join us."

"I'm not too young now."

"No, you aren't." Emily placed her palm over Vinnie's hand. "And I'm talking to you now."

Vinnie folded her arms and waited.

"It started four—no, now it's five days ago." She told Vinnie everything. How she had met Mr. Nobody in the meadow with the bees, and again at the smithy. She confided how attractive she thought Mr. Nobody was, and how much she had liked him.

After the body was found in the pond, Emily described the start of her investigation, her discovery that a carriage with an unusual wheel had been at the pond, and her suspicion that Mr. Nobody had been dragged into the water.

Vinnie gasped when she heard about Sam Wentworth's threats. Finally, Emily described the will that left a fortune to a dead son.

Emily stared at the table as she related her story. So much had happened in just a few days, and the investigation of it was so unsuitable for a young lady, particularly one with a tendency toward consumption.

When she was done, Emily looked up and saw that her sister was crying. "Vinnie, what's wrong?" she cried.

"That poor boy!" she sobbed. "To die alone and unremembered. Emily, everything you've done has been foolish and inappropriate—yet so right. He deserves justice."

Emily blinked back her own tears. How comforting her sister was. She was accustomed to undervaluing Vinnie but tonight she had proved her worth. Emily was no longer mourning alone.

"But this isn't something a proper young lady can undertake." Vinnie blew her nose into a scrap of cloth. "This is a job for the constable. Or Reverend Colton. Anybody else but you!"

Emily thought for a moment. "Well, we both know that I'm not a proper young lady. Besides, the constable has closed his case, and the reverend's only concern is Mr. Nobody's proper name. I'm the only one who cares about him. It has to be me." She stared at her sister until Vinnie nodded.

"I'm worried about you."

"I can take care of myself," Emily assured her, pushing away the memory of the muzzle of Mr. Ripley's shotgun. It had been an eventful day. "Vinnie, why did you come after me tonight?"

"A letter came today. Fortunately, I picked it up at the post office and not Mother." Vinnie went to the pantry and pulled a folded letter from behind a glass jar of dried currants. She handed it to Emily. "It's addressed to Miss Dickinson," she said, looking slightly embarrassed.

"Miss *E.* Dickinson," Emily pointed out. "And it's been opened."

"Is it an E?" Vinnie asked disingenuously. "I thought it might be an L. These mistakes happen."

"When you live with an inquisitive sister, they happen with great frequency." Emily glared at her sister as she unfolded the letter.

Dear Miss Dickinson,

Unfortunately, I have been called away to a prolonged confinement in Hadley, else I would deliver my information to your father in person.

I reexamined the unfortunate young man. There was no water in his lungs, which indicates that he was dead before he entered the pond. The cause of death is a stopped heart, a rare condition in a young, healthy man. The blueness under his fingernails is unaccountable, unless— and I hesitate to suggest this—poison was involved. Without knowing which poison, I cannot confirm this diagnosis.

I noticed a bruise has come up on his left cheek. If I had to guess, I would speculate that he was struck by a fist. I also noted cuts on the knuckles of his right hand, which indicate our unknown friend defended himself.

I will inform the authorities of my findings on my return, which should be Sunday at the latest. I am sure that your father does not want you to be involved any further in these dark matters, and I add my admonitions to his.

With regards,
Dr. Gridley

Emily leaned back against the stone hearth and let it bear the burden of her investigation, if only for a moment.

"What will you do?" Vinnie asked.

Straightening up, Emily said, "After Sunday, I shall be a prisoner in our comfortable house. I have until then." She stood up and began pacing around the kitchen table. "You'll help me?"

"Yes," Vinnie said without hesitation. "I wish I had met this Mr. Nobody. He sounds charming."

Emily scowled. "Why do you think I didn't mention him? Young men always prefer laughing with you to talking with me. If you were older, they wouldn't notice me at all."

"Unless they are very intelligent," Vinnie corrected. "Then they find me rather foolish and they admire you tremendously."

"I think Mr. Nobody might have admired me." Emily smiled sadly. "But we'll never know now."

"First things first," Vinnie said. "You must discover his name. It's ridiculous to keep calling him Mr. Nobody."

Swallowing hard, Emily nodded. "He might be a relation of Sam Wentworth's. Sam's nephew mentioned a cousin who arrived unexpectedly and who was supposed to be dead."

"Would that be the heir who was taken out of the will?" Vinnie asked.

"Possibly."

"That would put some noses out of joint," Vinnie said. "Wouldn't Mr. Wentworth lose a fortune?"

"Indeed. Some might say it's enough to drive a man to murder."

The word hung between them. *Murder.*

"But Mr. Nobody could just as easily be someone who has no connection at all to the Wentworths," Emily reminded her sister.

MICHAELA MACCOLL

"What shall we do next?" Vinnie looked at her sister expectantly.

"I'm not sure. All the odd facts I've accumulated seem like a tangled skein of wool—how on earth am I to unsnarl them?"

"Let us tackle each one in turn," Vinnie suggested simply.

Emily hugged her sister. "I have a list in my notebook."

"So that's what you've been writing!" Vinnie grabbed it from Emily's hand and opened it to the first page. The eagerness faded from her face.

"What is this, Emily? 'Clothes alien to himself'? 'Proportions distorted'? 'Blued flesh'? What does it all mean?"

Emily sighed. Why had she thought Vinnie would understand her jottings? She gave herself a shake; she would just have to explain in a way her sister could grasp. "Why was Mr. Nobody dressed so differently in death than in life?"

"Oh! Why didn't you just say so?" Vinnie asked. "You said he was very well dressed. A dandy, in fact."

Emily nodded. "But in the pond, he wore pants that were too short, and the sleeves of the shirt were abnormally long."

"That means the clothes were borrowed, doesn't it? If they were purchased for him, they would have fit better."

Emily looked at her sister fondly. Trust Vinnie to have special insight about clothing. "I asked Mr. Cutler if he knew who had bought the clothes, but he gave my questions short shrift."

"Did you describe them?"

"I didn't have to—there were stacks of them on the table at the store."

"But Emily, don't you see? We need to find a farmhand or a laborer with the dimensions you describe."

Emily thought about what her sister had said. "It's a good idea."

Vinnie was pleased. "What's next?"

Emily turned the page. "A wagon wheel with an unusual square pattern on its rim."

Vinnie grimaced. "Don't expect me to look at every wheel in town."

"Mr. Wentworth said he had just bought a new carriage. I wonder what the wheel is like?" Emily made a note.

She turned another page. "I found this odd flower." She held out the dried flower so her sister could see. "It was on the body."

Vinnie recoiled. "How did you find this?" she asked suspiciously. "You didn't search his body . . . did you?"

"Never mind." Emily hurried on. Perhaps Vinnie didn't need to know everything. "It's a clue, but I don't know how it fits in yet. I've never seen it before."

"Neither have I," Vinnie said.

Emily took a deep breath. "And most urgently, we need to identify the body. It may be James Wentworth—but what if it's someone else entirely?"

"Why don't we just ask Sam Wentworth?"

"Someone went to great lengths to disguise the body. If Sam had anything to do with this man's death, he'll just lie to me," Emily said. "Remember, he gets to keep a fortune if James is dead."

"What about the nephew, Henry? He seemed to be at odds with his uncle."

"What do you suggest I do? Confront him with the body? What an awkward conversation that would be!"

The girls pondered the question. Finally Vinnie said, "Emily, do you remember that time you said you had something to show me and you handed me a box? When I opened it up, it was a dead bird."

Emily shifted uncomfortably. "I said I was sorry, but the cat was killing birds and you didn't want to admit it. . . . Oh, I understand. If I confront Henry with Mr. Nobody's body, his face can't help but reveal the truth." She began scribbling in her notebook.

Vinnie watched for a while and then yawned. Twice. "Emily, I'm sleepy. I'm going to bed. Tell me your plan tomorrow."

Chewing on the end of her pencil, Emily didn't look up.

"Good night, Vinnie."

Vinnie kissed the top of Emily's head and headed for the back stairs.

"Vinnie?"

She paused, her hand on the wooden railing. "Yes?"

"Thank you for saving me tonight. It was brave of you. I'm an ungrateful wretch not to have said so immediately."

"You're the one who's brave, Emily," Vinnie said softly. "But you are very welcome."

Superiority to fate
Is difficult to learn.
'Tis not conferred by any,
But possible to earn.

CHAPTER 11

The next morning Emily paid for her sins by washing a mountain of laundry. She looked down at her red, chapped hands. With a sigh, she went back to rubbing her skirt on the ridged washing board. At least this was the last dress. Now she had only to wring the heavy, wet clothes and put them on the line to dry. She glanced toward the house and met her mother's watchful gaze from the kitchen window.

Vinnie came out of the chicken coop, wiping her dusty hands on her apron. She watched Emily for a few moments. She dipped her hands in the rinse water and picked up one of the dresses her sister had already washed. "I'll start wringing these," she said.

Her hands pushing hard against the fabric, Emily said, "No, Vinnie. Mother said I have to do this myself. I've taken advantage of you long enough."

From the kitchen door, their mother's voice was an uncanny echo of Emily's. "Vinnie, let Emily do the laundry. She's been far too lax lately, and you've done more than your share."

"Mother, I don't mind," Vinnie called. "And I want to go for a walk with Emily later, so the quicker she finishes, the sooner we can go."

Mrs. Dickinson shrugged and closed the door.

After checking that their mother was out of earshot, Vinnie asked eagerly, "Emily, have you thought of anything else we should investigate?"

The aching in Emily's shoulder seemed to ease. Vinnie's help with both the laundry and her quest for justice was like a tonic. "The will. Mr. Wentworth has a sister, Violet Langston, from Boston."

"That doesn't do us much good," Vinnie complained.

"The file showed a new address for the Langstons in Amherst." Emily smiled slyly. "On College Street."

Vinnie looked alert, like one of her cats spying a bird. "Ursula Langston's mother?" Ursula had recently become a classmate of theirs at Amherst Academy.

"It must be!" Emily said. "I think it's time for an intimate conversation with Ursula."

"But you can't stand her," Vinnie pointed out as she wrung the water out of the last dress.

"That's not true," Emily protested.

"Didn't you say all she thought about was fashion and society?"

"I did, but in spite of that she could be interesting. She was wonderful in botany class. You should see her herbarium."

Their botany instructor had encouraged the girls to keep herbariums, handmade books that categorized every flower and plant they saw on their botanical walks.

"Emily," Vinnie said excitedly. "Why don't you look for that odd flower in your herbarium?"

Emily groaned and rubbed her temples with her wet fingers. "I did this morning. It isn't in there."

"Maybe Ursula can help with that," Vinnie said. "What else will you ask her?"

"Ursula must know what happened with her uncle's will." Emily explained. "Her mother must have inherited a lot of money."

"But the Langstons are rich," Vinnie said. "Or, at least, they always seemed to be."

"Perhaps they didn't need the legacy, but perhaps they did. I think I'll visit the Amherst Savings Bank today.

Cousin Stanley should be there and I'll bring him some of my gingerbread."

"But he won't tell you about the Langstons' finances, will he?"

Emily threw a dress over the washing line and began to clip it in place. "I've found that when you engage people in conversation, they often tell you more than they intend. That's why I avoid idle conversation whenever I can—I like to keep my secrets!"

"You are entirely too secretive," Vinnie said with a glower. "Now let's finish this laundry so we can get started."

With Vinnie's help, the rest of the laundry was on the line before noon. The sisters went inside to remove their aprons and put on bonnets to shelter their faces from the sun. Mrs. Dickinson sat in her rocking chair near the window, reading the *Hampshire Gazette*.

"There's a horrible story about two children in Michigan who ate a toadstool instead of a mushroom. They died immediately."

Emily and Vinnie exchanged glances. "Fortunately, Mother, we know the difference between the two," Emily said.

"You needn't worry about us," Vinnie chimed in.

"I always worry," Mrs. Dickinson said. She looked up and noticed their bonnets. "Where are you two going?"

"Just around the shops," Vinnie answered.

"I thought I might bring Cousin Stanley some gingerbread at the bank," Emily said virtuously. "His wife is away, and I'm sure he would appreciate some home baking."

"That is very thoughtful of you," her mother said, eyeing her suspiciously. "Especially since you have been so remiss about your duties lately."

"Mother, I will do anything to make up for my thoughtlessness."

"If only you really meant that."

"But I do," Emily assured her.

A smile played on Mrs. Dickinson's lips. "Excellent. The Sewing Circle is coming here tomorrow, and you may help me host it. "

"That's not fair!" Emily complained. "I've been irresponsible, but I don't deserve that!"

"Mother!" Vinnie echoed. "You are disciplining Emily by forcing her to entertain. What will you do if she is really naughty? Make her to go to a dance?"

"Vinnie, please don't suggest any more punishment," Emily said. "The Sewing Circle is quite deadly enough."

"What am I to do with both of you?" Mrs. Dickinson sank into a chair and blew away a lock of her dark hair that had escaped her bun. "Vinnie, stop teasing your sister— it's not attractive. And Emily, spare me your flippancy.

Someday you'll be married with your own household and you will have to entertain, just as I do."

"But does it have to be the Sewing Circle?" Emily cried. "All those women do is gossip." A thought struck her. Very casually, as though the suggestion were of no importance, she asked, "But if I have to, perhaps I could also invite a friend from school?"

"Who?" Mrs. Dickinson asked, wary of Emily's sudden capitulation.

"Ursula Langston."

"Must it be the Langstons?" Mrs. Dickinson sighed. "We can't invite Ursula without her mother, who has a terrible reputation. She's been here only six months, and she's already tried to worm her way into every group of consequence."

"Ursula invited me to tea once." Emily was exaggerating. What Ursula had actually said was that perhaps one day all the girls from their botany class should have tea. "It is only right that I reciprocate."

"Very well." Her mother sounded unenthusiastic.

"They may not come," Emily said. "It's very short notice for an invitation."

"Then let us hope that they have another engagement." With a sharp nod, Mrs. Dickinson started to leave the room. At the door, she turned back and said, "I'm glad to see that you are taking your duties more seriously."

After their mother was gone, Vinnie turned to Emily. "Well done! She didn't suspect a thing."

⫸✳⫷

Emily led the way up the hill toward the Common. "I'll go to the bank," she said.

"And I'll find out where Mr. Nobody's clothes came from," Vinnie said. Even though there was no one nearby, she lowered her voice. "Emily, mightn't it be useful to see them for myself?"

"Absolutely not," Emily answered sharply. "I don't want you going anywhere near the church. You shouldn't see. . . . It's rather . . . upsetting."

"It's not as if we both haven't seen lots of bodies," Vinnie pouted. "We've sat with more corpses than I can count."

"This one is different," Emily said.

Vinnie looked searchingly in Emily's face. "I mustn't forget that he was your friend."

Emily shook herself, as if to repel Vinnie's pity. "You'll have to rely on the description I gave you. And be careful. We don't know how Mr. Nobody died yet."

"I'll be ever so subtle," Vinnie promised.

"Bless you." Emily embraced her.

Vinnie's navy dress was trimmed with red and looked very well on her. She started toward Cutler's with a confidence that Emily envied.

Trying to imitate her, Emily walked to the Amherst Savings Bank and pushed open the tall oak door. The first person she saw was Cousin Stanley behind the long counter.

Spying her, he beamed. "Emily!"

"Hello, cousin."

"How is your mother?"

"Fairly well, although the heat brings on her neuralgia."

"The heat—or her daughters' mischief-making?"

Emily shrugged.

"What can I do for you today? Do you need a loan?" He laughed at his own joke.

"I've brought some gingerbread for you."

He beamed. "Thank you, my dear; that's very thoughtful. And your gingerbread is wonderful."

"I've used a new recipe," Emily fibbed. "My friend, Ursula Langston, gave it to me. Perhaps you know her family?"

"The Langstons? Of course I do."

"Isn't it lovely how they came into a legacy recently?"

"The money came just in time, too." He nodded sagely. "That Charles Langston is a sly one—sharp at a bargain and even sharper at cutting corners. But all of his tricks wouldn't have saved him from bankruptcy."

"They weren't always wealthy?" Emily asked casually.

He shook his head vigorously. "They're very good at keeping up appearances."

Emily was thoughtful. "That's very important to some people."

"My dear, you have no idea. There are families in this town who would kill to keep their good reputation."

His words echoed in the empty bank; not that Emily needed to hear them more than once. She quickly said good-bye and went outside. She couldn't wait to tell her sister what she had discovered.

"Emily!" Vinnie came rushing up, her pretty face flushed with excitement. "I found him!"

Several ladies, staid and respectable with their shopping baskets, looked askance at the girls, and Emily was certain they would inform Mother that Vinnie had made a spectacle of herself in public.

"Lower your voice, or all of Amherst will know you have a new beau," Emily said loudly. Better to start a false rumor than have their mother find out the truth.

Vinnie crinkled her nose, as she often did when she was confused. "A beau? What do you mean?"

"Never mind. Who did you find?"

"The owner of your Mr. Nobody's clothes. He's a freed slave named Horace Goodman."

"How did you find him?"

"Mr. Cutler's delivery boy recognized the description. But that's not the most interesting thing. He's a handyman. And who do you think he works for?"

"Not..."

"The Langstons!" Vinnie supplied. "Isn't it odd how everything we discover seems to come back to them?"

"Good work," Emily said, although she found her sister's triumphant air irritating. This was her mystery. Vinnie was involved only because she had blackmailed Emily. "We must talk to him, but preferably not at the Langstons'."

Vinnie preened. "He also works at the Amherst House on Wednesdays, and he takes his dinner in the tavern. He's there now."

"Let's go," Emily said, starting for the hotel.

"But we aren't permitted to go there by ourselves!"

Emily didn't hesitate. "Some things are more important than propriety."

The Amherst House was the best hotel in town, and its tavern was a popular destination with students and workingmen alike. There was a ladies' dining room where the Dickinsons dined occasionally, but Emily and Vinnie had never been in the noisy bar. In fact, their father was a prominent member of the Temperance Union, whose goal was to close every bar in town.

Emily pushed open the swinging door, while Vinnie hung back. As the patrons noticed them, silence spread like redcurrant juice on a white tablecloth. The barman glared at them and demanded what they wanted.

Vinnie was speechless, mortified at finding herself the object of so many masculine stares. Emily spoke up and asked for Horace Goodman.

The barman gave them a curious look. "He's in the back."

"Thank you," Emily said, grabbing Vinnie's hand to drag her along.

Horace Goodman was seated at a small table in the corner. His skin was dark, and his hair was a wiry gray. He was big—so big that his long arms seemed to need another table to accommodate their length. He was eating a meat pie and mumbling to himself.

"Mr. Goodman?" Emily asked. "May I speak with you?"

He pushed himself away from the table, his eyes darting around like a hunted animal's. Emily noticed that they were rimmed red. When he saw it was only two young girls, he seemed to relax.

"What do you want?" he asked in a tired voice.

"Why did you gave your shirt, pants, and boots to a man who turned up dead in my pond?" Emily asked.

Vinnie shot Emily a startled glance, but Emily thought bluntness might startle some truth out of Horace.

"I didn't hurt anybody," Horace cried.

"I didn't say you did," Emily said. "But as I already know a portion of the story, don't you think you should explain the whole?"

Horace was breathing quickly, and his giant fists clenched and unclenched on the table. "I didn't hurt anybody."

"I know you didn't," Emily said sternly. "But you must tell me what happened."

"I don't want any trouble," he muttered. "I just do as I'm bid."

"Did someone ask you for your clothes? Or to move a body, perhaps?" Emily asked shrewdly. Vinnie gasped.

Horace stared at her like a mouse might greet a hawk. Suddenly he panicked and stood up. He was short, especially compared to his long arms. Emily saw how easy it must have been for Vinnie to link the oddly proportioned clothing to its owner.

"Stay away from me." He brushed past them roughly, almost knocking Vinnie down. Emily steadied her sister and watched him push through the patrons and run out the door.

The barman glared at them again. Emily and Vinnie took his meaning and quietly followed Horace outside. He was nowhere to be seen, but the townspeople in the Common were chattering about his abrupt departure.

On their way home, Emily mused, "That certainly looked like a guilty conscience."

"Indeed," Vinnie agreed. "But for what? Do you think he killed Mr. Nobody?"

"And then dressed the body in his own clothes? Why lay a trail that returns to him?"

"But he knows something."

Emily nodded. "And it frightens him terribly."

Her fingers fumbled at her work, —
Her needle would not go:
What ailed so smart a little maid
It puzzled me to know

CHAPTER 12

The next day dawned with a rainstorm that turned the dirt roads to a mud that would easily ruin a lady's shoes. Several of the guests sent their regrets, but Ursula Langston and her mother arrived precisely on time. Both were dressed far more fashionably than the other women.

Mrs. Dickinson was frigidly polite. "Mrs. Langston, what a lovely dress," she said.

"Why, thank you. My husband had it sent from Paris. At enormous expense." Mrs. Langston had the same pale blue eyes as her brother, Sam Wentworth, but fashion had altered her into an entirely foreign creature. "It was an extravagance, but I love pretty things." She looked at Mrs. Dickinson's plain gown. "But I do admire how the ladies in Amherst don't worry overmuch about the latest fashions."

Mrs. Dickinson's eyes narrowed, but she was too polite to reply in kind. She made the introductions. "I don't believe you know Mrs. Hitchcock and Mrs. Gilbert."

Since Mrs. Hitchcock was the wife of the president of Amherst College and Mrs. Gilbert's husband owned the bank, Mrs. Langston was delighted to make their prestigious acquaintance.

Ursula's quick glance made it obvious that she didn't think much of the younger Dickinsons' dresses. For their part, Emily and Vinnie were unobtrusively sizing up her ensemble. Ursula was only a year older than Emily, but her polka-dotted dress with a daring neckline showed off her shoulders and made her seem at least eighteen. She wore a choker of the same fabric. Her sausage curls cascaded down both sides of her face. Emily conceded that Ursula looked very attractive, but thought the rigidity of a corset was too high a price to pay for appearance's sake.

Mrs. Dickinson led her guests into the parlor, where seven chairs were arranged in a wide circle. The older ladies claimed the seats by the window to take advantage of the limited daylight.

"Your house is lovely, Mrs. Dickinson," Mrs. Langston said. "The brocade on this chair is so unusual. Was it expensive?"

"It was a gift from my father when I married," Mrs. Dickinson said, her face pink.

"As old as that?" Mrs. Langston rubbed her fingertips on the patterned fabric. "Ah, now I see that it is quite worn. The light in here is not very good, or I would have noticed it earlier."

For a moment, Mrs. Dickinson's famed composure deserted her. She took refuge in arranging the work of the sewing circle. "Ladies," she said, raising her voice. "Our task today is to make baby clothes for the Irish families working in the factory."

Mrs. Hitchcock said, "Those women. Always too many babies and not enough money."

"Charity, Mrs. Hitchcock," Mrs. Dickinson reminded her. "It is our duty to help the less fortunate."

"We do seem to sew an inordinate number of baby clothes," murmured Mrs. Gilbert.

Emily, Ursula, and Vinnie hovered by the door as their elders got settled.

"Sit down, Emily," her mother said.

"May we be excused for a few minutes to show Ursula my herbarium?"

"I'd like to see it," Ursula said politely.

"Emily, I'm sure your herbarium is very nice," Mrs. Langston said, "but Miss Phelps said that Ursula's was the best in the class."

"Ursula, you and Emily were in Miss Phelps's botany class together, weren't you?" Mrs. Dickinson said.

Mrs. Langston turned eagerly to the other ladies. "Ursula received top marks in botany. She's so clever that she makes almost all our little remedies. We hardly need to visit the pharmacist. She dries peppermint for a tea that takes away my headaches, prepares chamomile for compresses, and recently began making her uncle's heart medicine from flowers in the garden."

"How useful," Mrs. Hitchcock said drily.

Emily had a grin on her face as she led the way upstairs. Ursula's face was bright red. "I must apologize for my mother," she said once they reached the bedroom. "To her, a random thought might as well be spoken aloud. And of course, she's been hoping for an invitation from the mighty Dickinson family since we moved here."

Emily and Vinnie exchanged glances. "Don't apologize," Emily said. "You *are* very talented in botany. In fact, I have a plant I can't identify, and I was hoping you could help me."

"If I can," Ursula said.

Ursula and Vinnie sat on the bed while Emily fetched the heavy herbarium. They turned the pages. Emily had begun well, pasting in a variety of plants and labeling them with their Latin names and origins. As she got toward the end of the pages, the plants were shoved in haphazardly—some not even secured to the page.

Ursula leafed through, saying very little. Emily remembered how there had been an unspoken competition between them during the class. Miss Phelps had praised Emily's herbarium, and suddenly Ursula had worked furiously to make her book twice as nice as Emily's.

"Where is this unknown plant?" Ursula asked.

Emily removed her notebook from her bodice, opened it to the last page, and pulled out the flower. "This is my mystery flower," she said in a casual voice.

Ursula took it and laid it on an empty page in the herbarium, studying it intently. "Where did you find it?" She finally looked up, a small smile on her lips.

"I can't recall," Emily lied. "It's pretty, but I can't quite place it. The petals have an odd soft texture, and the stem is more wood than plant. What kind of flower is it?"

"It's not a flower at all!" Ursula said triumphantly. "It's an Indian pipe, and it's a fungus."

"I remember now," Emily nodded. "I'd never seen one, but Miss Phelps described them."

"Miss Phelps took me on special walks. Just the two of us." Ursula shot a triumphant glance at Emily. "Once we went to a place called Amethyst Brook. There were dozens of Indian pipes there under the dead trees. They feast on the decay of other plants."

Vinnie shivered. "How unnatural!" But Emily could see that she was just as fascinated as Emily.

"Amethyst Brook," Emily repeated. "I've never been there, but I'll have to visit."

"Emily! Vinnie!" It was their mother, grown impatient downstairs.

"Coming, Mother!" The girls returned to the sewing circle.

"Ursula, sit with me," Emily said as she settled on a sofa next to the fireplace. She pulled out a plain baby gown from her sewing basket and fastened an embroidery hoop around the front of the garment. "I haven't seen you since term ended. How have you been keeping yourself?"

Ursula looked bored. "Mother took me to New York to buy some new gowns."

"New dresses!" Vinnie sighed with longing. "Mother insists that we cut our own patterns. The dressmaker comes in two weeks to sew the dresses for us."

From across the circle, Mrs. Dickinson called out. "Remember, Lavinia, to make your own clothes is a virtuous use of your time. And if our circumstances should ever change, you would know how to economize."

"Is Mr. Dickinson's law practice so precarious?" Mrs. Langston asked, oblivious to the raised eyebrows of the other ladies.

"Of course not," Mrs. Dickinson said. "But I believe my girls should be trained for any eventuality."

"*The Frugal Housewife* again," Vinnie said.

Ursula looked puzzled. "Who is that?"

"It's not a person, it's Mother's second bible." Emily explained. "The first is Scripture, the second is Mrs. Child's *The Frugal Housewife*."

"And you shouldn't make just your clothes," Vinnie said. "Soap, cheese, anything that would be more convenient to purchase, *The Frugal Housewife* would have you make yourself."

Ursula looked horrified. "It sounds deadly."

Emily laughed. "Remember the passage about young women? It seems we should not waste our time with education, because that only prepares us for a life of idleness. A diligent mother would school us in the domestic arts."

"And to think I always envied you!" Ursula laughed. "Mother would rather die than have me wear homemade clothes."

Emily and Vinnie exchanged amused looks.

Mrs. Hitchcock spoke loudly, as if to change the subject. "Has everyone seen," she paused dramatically, "the Body?"

"Don't speak of it, dear," Mrs. Dickinson said. "I've forbidden the girls to even think of it."

"Our maid discovered it!" Vinnie said.

Mrs. Hitchcock leaned forward, her mouth half-open. "Of course! He was found on your property, wasn't he?" She playfully tapped Mrs. Dickinson's arm with her embroidery hoop. "The whole town is talking of it. I went to have a peek, but I had never seen the poor man before."

In a high-pitched voice, Mrs. Langston said, "Oh, was a body found? I hadn't heard anything about it."

"If you want to see, you had better hurry," Mrs. Gilbert said. "He'll have to be buried soon. I made my husband bring me—I was afraid I would swoon. But the poor boy looked very natural. And so good-looking."

Emily felt a sickness in her stomach.

Mrs. Dickinson shook her head sharply. "Please, not in front of the children. They are already fascinated with death. I recall last year when Emily's friend Sophia died—she insisted on staying at her deathbed for days. Emily's health suffered for months afterward."

There was silence in the room as the ladies contemplated Emily, who blushed to the roots of her red hair, seething that her mother would bring up poor Sophia.

Mrs. Hitchcock broke the silence after a few moments and asked Mrs. Langston, "Are you enjoying your stay in Amherst?"

Mrs. Langston's cheeks were flushed, but she seemed to welcome the change of subject. "It's quite wet, isn't it? I daresay it rained in Boston, but I don't recall there ever being so much mud in Beacon Hill."

"You lived in Beacon Hill?" Mrs. Dickinson asked.

With a nostalgic sigh, Mrs. Langston nodded. "Our house was so convenient and our neighbors were quite famous." She waited, and when no question came, she added, "Of course, it would be unladylike to tell you their names."

Emily bit her lip and settled back to watch her mother deal with her guest's unusual manners.

"Beacon Street is such a desirable address," Mrs. Dickinson said. "Charles Street has lovely shops."

"You've been there?" Mrs. Langston asked, looking slightly alarmed.

"You may not know, but my husband used to be the representative for Amherst to the Massachusetts Legislature. Did you live near the State House?"

"No. We don't care overmuch for politicians. My husband says they are all thieves and liars." She laughed. "He says they aren't to be trusted."

Emily nearly stabbed her mouth with her sewing needle when she covered her lips to prevent a laugh from escaping. Vinnie's giggle was audible, while Ursula, mortified, stared fixedly at her embroidery.

Mrs. Dickinson blinked. Finally, she asked, "What brought you to Amherst?"

"We didn't have much choice," Ursula muttered.

"Hush, Ursula!" Mrs. Langston snapped.

Emily glanced from mother to daughter.

"My brother lives here," Mrs. Langston said. "We had lost touch, and I thought it important to spend some time with him."

Emily carefully fixed her needle to the fabric and leaned forward. "Do you have a large family? Any other brothers?"

Mrs. Langston glared at Emily. "Not any longer," she said sharply.

"I'm sorry; I didn't realize it was a sensitive subject." By now all the ladies were staring at Mrs. Langston.

Shifting her weight in her seat, Mrs. Langston said, "I had another brother, Jeremiah, but he passed away recently."

"How terribly sad," Emily said. "How did he die?"

Mrs. Dickinson inhaled sharply. "Emily, enough of these personal questions. Where are your manners?"

"He was killed while prospecting in the Dakotas," Mrs. Langston said.

"Did he have any children?" Emily probed.

"No, unfortunately his only son died young." Mrs. Langston pursed her lips and glared at Emily. "And now, if you don't mind, I'd rather discuss something less upsetting."

"Emily, enough," Mrs. Dickinson agreed. "I declare you are becoming quite morbid."

Emily could have screamed with frustration. How was she going to discover anything if her mother kept cutting the conversation short? She jabbed her needle hard through the fabric and inadvertently stabbed the fleshy part of her thumb. She stared as a drop of red blood dripped onto the white fabric and spread like a plague across her careful stitches.

I measure every grief I meet

With analytic eyes;

I wonder if it weighs like mine,

Or has an easier size.

CHAPTER 13

"Emily, you're bleeding," Vinnie exclaimed.

"It's nothing," Emily said. She noticed that Ursula was staring at the bloody marks on the fabric, her face pale.

A knock on the door rescued Emily from being the center of attention. "I'll answer the door." She put aside her embroidery and jumped up.

"Not even a maid to greet your guests?" Violet Langston murmured, just loud enough for Emily to hear.

"Mother!" Ursula whispered.

Sucking on her pricked thumb, Emily left the parlor. A gust of wind tugged the oak door out of her hand so it slammed against the wall. A young man wearing oilskins stood there. His face was all too familiar.

"You!" Emily said.

He peered into the dark hallway. When he saw Emily, he stepped back into the rain. "You! What are you doing here?"

"This is my home," Emily said.

Suddenly Mrs. Langston's shrill voice broke the spell. "Henry! Come in out of the rain. What are you doing here?"

Henry pulled back his hood and, with a wary glance at Emily, leaned forward to kiss his mother on the cheek. "I arrived on the stage this morning. Father told me you were here, so I came to fetch you. I hope I'm not too early."

"And who is this?" Mrs. Dickinson had followed Mrs. Langston into the hallway.

Mrs. Langston beamed. "Mrs. Dickinson and Miss Emily Dickinson, let me introduce you to my son, Henry Langston. He has just arrived from New Haven."

She paused, waiting for someone to ask. Emily finally obliged. "Do you go to Yale, Mr. Langston?"

"Yes, I'm studying law." He gave her a quick conspiratorial grin that thanked her for humoring his snobbish mother.

"And you only arrived today?" Emily pressed, giving him a hard look. His grin faded, and she could see a flush creeping up the back of his neck.

Ursula appeared in the crowded hallway. Seeing her brother, she squealed and ran into his embrace. "Henry!"

"Ursula, you'll get your dress wet," he said, laughing.

Emily felt a pang for her own absent brother. For the first time, she envied Ursula.

Mrs. Langston performed the introductions.

"It's a pleasure to meet you all." Henry glanced outside. "But as I think the weather is clearing, I should bring my mother and sister home right away."

For a few minutes, confusion reigned as coats were donned and umbrellas lost and found. Henry held the door open for his mother and sister. With him at their elbows, they picked their way down the muddy path into a waiting carriage. Emily stayed in the doorway while the other guests returned to the parlor.

"Mr. Langston," Emily called after him. He closed the door of the carriage and came halfway up the path, almost as if he were keeping a safe distance from her.

"Yes, Miss Dickinson?"

She slipped on wooden clogs over her slippers and walked out into the rain, sheltered only by her inadequate umbrella. Her heels sank into the mud. "Now that we know each other's names, perhaps we should be honest about a few other facts."

"I beg your pardon?" He avoided looking directly at her.

"We both know that you didn't arrive in Amherst today," Emily said.

He glanced at the carriage. "It's not necessary to mention that to my mother, is it?"

"Of course not," Emily said. "Not if you meet me at the church at three this afternoon." She pointed to the spire of the First Congregational Church up the hill. "I have something to show you."

"I'm not sure I can get away," he said.

"Then I'm not sure I can keep what I know to myself," Emily replied.

"I'll try to be there," he said grudgingly, stepping through the mud back to the carriage. He swung himself up to the box seat and took up the reins.

After the carriage had turned onto the road, Emily couldn't take her eyes off its tracks unspooling before her. They were quickly filling up with mud, but inside the imprint left by the right side wheel, Emily noticed a square mark.

"So there, Vinnie," she murmured to herself. "We didn't need to go looking for the wheel. It rolled right to our front door."

✳❊✳

MICHAELA MACCOLL

Henry Langston was waiting at the top of the steps to the church when Emily arrived. They were alone—the rain had kept most of Amherst indoors. Neither was inclined to break the awkward silence.

"Why did you ask me to meet you here?" Henry finally asked.

"Why did you agree to come?" she countered.

He said nothing.

"You were in Sam Wentworth's house yesterday," Emily said finally. "And possibly a few days before that."

"So? I'm his nephew." He leaned against the wall, reminding her of Mr. Nobody when he had reclined against the wooden post in the stable. "You were the one trespassing."

"Why did you lie to your mother?"

He stiffened. "If I choose to spend time with my uncle without my mother knowing, that's my affair."

"Were you there five days ago?" Emily felt like a lawyer in court, trying to pin down a recalcitrant witness.

"Why are you asking all these questions?" he complained. "I agreed to meet you because I was curious. You upset my uncle badly, and I want to know why."

"I'll explain, but first please tell me . . . five days ago?"

"I was there, but my uncle was in Northampton purchasing the carriage you saw this morning."

"And did you give someone some of your uncle's honeycomb?"

"How do you know that?" He stepped back. "Miss Dickinson, I begin to think perhaps you are a witch!" The expression on his face reminded her of Mr. Nobody's—but this young man lacked Mr. Nobody's insouciant charm.

"Mr. Langston, I need the answer to my question. It's more important than you can possibly guess."

He looked around, as though he was afraid they were being watched. "I gave some honey to my cousin," he admitted.

"Is he your age? And of your build and complexion?"

"When we were younger, people commented we could have been brothers."

Emily nodded. Hadn't she been taken aback by the uncanny resemblance? "His name?" Her words hung in the humid air, their simplicity demanding an answer.

"I must insist you explain what my family's private business is to you," Mr. Langston said, bristling with suspicion.

Emily took a deep breath. "I'm so sorry to have to do this." She turned to pull open the church door. Automatically, he stepped forward to hold it open. In silence, she led him to the basement vestry.

Her plan had seemed so simple the other night in the kitchen, but now she wasn't so sure of herself. If her deductions were correct, she was about to subject Mr. Langston to a dreadful ordeal.

MICHAELA MACCOLL

His eyes shifted rapidly from one corner of the dim interior to another until they lit on the table. "Is that a body?" he asked.

Emily reflected that he might be the only person in Amherst who didn't know about the body in the vestry. News must not often reach Sam Wentworth's farm.

Without a word, she led him to the makeshift bier. Studying Mr. Langston's countenance, she gently lifted the cloth from the corpse's face.

Mr. Langston gasped and recoiled. "Cousin James!"

"James," Emily repeated, her suspicions confirmed. Finally her mysterious friend had a name, and she felt a weight lift from her shoulders. James Wentworth. The dead cousin, miraculously resurrected, only to perish again.

Henry Langston was staring at the body. His face was pale, and Emily could see beads of sweat on his forehead that had nothing to do with the sticky weather. How do you read guilt or innocence in a man's expression? He seemed shocked, and that boded well. Besides, Emily knew for a fact that Mr. Nobody, or James as she should call him now, had been alive and well when he left his cousin, honeycomb in pocket.

He stepped closer to get a better look. Then he whirled around and turned on Emily. "How dare you not warn me that my own cousin lay here?"

He loomed over her, and she stepped back involuntarily. Emily defended herself. "I wasn't sure; I only suspected."

"What is he doing here? He was fine on Friday." He rubbed his damp forehead with the back of his hand. "I have to tell my parents that we've lost him again."

"Again?" Emily asked, although she suspected she understood very well.

"We received word of his death months ago. You could have knocked me down with a feather when he showed up at Uncle's door." He groaned. "This will kill Mother."

"She doesn't know?" Emily asked, watching him closely. "What about Ursula?"

"Did they act as if they knew James was dead? Of course Ursula and my mother don't know." He sank onto a bench against the whitewashed wall. "How did he come to be here? Why hasn't my family been told?"

"No one knew his name. He's here to be identified. The whole town has come through looking at him, but no one recognized him."

"The entire town?" He looked over to the body, as if trying to envision a line of sober townspeople. "But I'm not surprised that no one knew him. He only came to Amherst a few times to visit Uncle. And that was several years ago."

"Your mother . . . "

"Would never think of looking at a body—she'd consider it vulgar. And Ursula is much too squeamish."

Emily nodded. This rang true. When Ursula had seen Emily bleeding from her little pinprick, she had nearly fainted. "Mr. Langston, there are many mysteries surrounding your cousin's death."

His eyes went to the body. "Do you mean to say that this was not an accidental death?"

"I fear not."

He swallowed hard and looked pale. "In that case, I need to consult with my family. We may possibly need legal advice."

She remembered that he was studying law.

"First you must talk to me," Emily said firmly. "Your cousin was my friend, and I need to discover how he died. And why."

"It's none of your concern . . . " He did a double take. "If you knew him, why is he lying here nameless?"

"We were friends," Emily admitted, "but I didn't know his name."

"That's ridiculous!" His tone was razor-sharp.

"I know, but it's true." To Emily's horror, she felt the tears welling up. She waved her hand in front of her eyes in a futile attempt to stop them.

With automatic courtesy, Mr. Langston reached into his coat and handed her a handkerchief. When she looked up, she saw that his eyes were also filled with tears. Wordlessly, she handed it back to him.

"Miss Dickinson . . . " His whole demeanor was gentler now, as though her tears had dissolved his anger.

"Emily."

"Emily, I can see you cared about James . . . " He had to stop and clear his throat. "Naturally, I find that a point in your favor."

She sniffed and dabbed at the corners of her eyes. "Then please, Mr. Langston, tell me everything you know."

The only secret people keep

Is Immortality.

CHAPTER 14

They sat on the steps of the church, under the porch, watching the rain fall in gentle sheets. Finally, he began to speak.

"My mother has two brothers. Sam, whom you met..."

"And a courteous gentleman he was, Mr. Langston," Emily said drily.

"Call me Henry," he said with a wry smile. "And to be fair, you were stealing my uncle's honey. He takes that personally." With a tightening of her heart, Emily saw that Henry was even more like his cousin than she had thought.

"My mother's other brother was Jeremiah. Sam is a simple soul. Give him his orchard and hives and he's content. Jeremiah was restless, never staying in one place, always traveling to find his fortune somewhere else. He would disappear for months or years at a time."

"And did he make his fortune?" Emily asked, although she had seen a list of Jeremiah's extensive securities and bank accounts.

"Several times!" Henry chuckled. "And often lost it just as quickly. It drove Father to distraction. He would beg Jeremiah to let him invest it, a safeguard against old age. But Jeremiah said he never intended to grow old and that my father could take his advice and go to the devil." Henry suddenly recalled he was speaking to a lady. "I beg your pardon."

"Your mother mentioned that he passed away," Emily prompted, impatient with the social niceties.

He nodded. "We knew he was in the Dakotas. He got lucky and made a fortune. And then we heard nothing for eighteen months. My mother was beside herself with worry."

Having met the shallow Mrs. Langston, Emily doubted this, but she held her tongue.

"About six months ago, we heard he was dead."

Emily calculated. "That's when your family moved here from Boston."

"Yes."

"Why?" Emily asked.

"Mother said she wanted to go to Amherst to be near her only surviving brother, but she really wanted to be close by while my uncle's estate was settled."

"Did your family need the money?" Emily asked, braced for a rebuff for asking such an indiscreet question.

But Henry stood up, walked to the end of the porch, and looked out at the rain for a few moments. Finally, he came back to her and said, "My father was in the midst of a financial crisis in Boston. I was forced to leave school, and we had to sell the house. And Mother was concerned about Ursula. She had fallen into a fast set in Boston and was accumulating her own debts at an alarming rate."

Emily, despite her oft-protested dislike of gossip, was dying to know more about Ursula's goings-on. Feeling like a wren who had to choose between two juicy worms, she forced herself to concentrate on the story of Jeremiah Wentworth. "So your mother and Sam inherited a fortune?"

"They split everything between them. And I was able to go back to Yale."

Trying to study his face without being obvious, Emily asked the essential question. "Jeremiah had an heir, didn't he? A son. Your cousin, James."

"Uncle Jeremiah had married a girl in the wilds of Texas. She died in childbirth. Jeremiah never had much interest in being a father, so he sent James to school as soon as he was old enough."

"But he never stayed at school very long." Emily remembered how Mr. Nobody—she would have to get used to calling him James—had scorned the academic life.

"He spoke of that to you?" Henry smiled reminiscently. "He ran away time after time. Finally when he was sixteen he disappeared for good. We thought he might have gone out West, or signed up for a merchant ship."

"I think it was a ship," Emily said. "He spoke of the sea."

"Of course," Henry said. "He loved to travel."

"Tell me what happened then."

"Then we heard he was dead." Henry's story had come to an abrupt halt.

"How?"

He thought and then shook his head. "I don't know. My mother wrote me at school."

"When was this?"

"Last Christmas. But she told me he had died months earlier. Before his father."

The sequence of events seemed suspicious to Emily. And if her suspicions were correct, it was precisely the sequence of events that mattered.

Jeremiah, the rich brother, was out in the wilds of the Dakotas. He could die at any time. James, his son and

MICHAELA MACCOLL

rightful heir, was—who knew where? In any event, he was unlikely to return. A simple codicil to Jeremiah's will stating that his son was dead meant that the remaining heirs, the Langstons and Sam Wentworth, would get their money that much sooner. If Jeremiah or James ever turned up alive, an unscrupulous clerk could simply destroy the codicil. It was diabolically clever.

"But the rightful heir to Jeremiah's fortune was very much alive," Emily pointed out. "James was eating honeycomb Friday last."

"It was a shock, let me tell you." Henry clasped his hands and began cracking his knuckles. "I hadn't seen him since we were about thirteen—but I recognized him right away. I was glad it was I who met him and not Uncle. He has a heart condition; the shock might have killed him."

"Was your meeting amicable?" Emily asked, her eyes narrowed as she waited for his answer.

"Of course it was." Henry sounded almost puzzled. "I was delighted to see that he was alive."

"Even if it meant the loss of your family's inheritance?"

"What kind of cold-blooded monster do you think I am?" he burst out. "Besides, it wouldn't have mattered. Uncle Jeremiah must have heard his son was dead too. He changed his will to remove James as a beneficiary, leaving my mother and Uncle Sam to inherit."

That was the codicil Emily had found in her father's office. "So James came back to life—and found you and your family in possession of his inheritance?"

"It was an honest mistake." Henry pronounced each syllable deliberately. "I told James so. There was no one to blame."

Staring at his face, Emily searched for signs of guilty knowledge. "You truly believe that?"

He glared at her. "Of course it was a mistake! Even if James had gone to the law, we would have reached some sort of compromise. There was plenty to go around. My Uncle Sam refused to touch his portion anyway."

"Why?" Emily found that most suspicious of all. Surely only a guilty conscience would cause someone to refuse a fortune?

Henry shrugged. "He doesn't need much."

"But luckily for your family, James died again. Suddenly." Emily let the bald words, with all their sinister implications, hang in the humid air.

Henry was silent, and Emily could see that his fists were clenched. Finally he glanced sideways and asked in a low voice, "How did he die?"

"He was found floating in our pond," Emily said.

"Drowned?" The tension drained out of him. "So it was an accident?"

"Possibly," Emily said. "But don't you think it's an odd coincidence that my father, Edward Dickinson, was Jeremiah Wentworth's lawyer—and Jeremiah's son ends up dead in our pond?"

"Nothing is more common than drowning," Henry said. "Why were you being so melodramatic with your talk of mysterious circumstances?" He stood up and brushed several raindrops off his trousers. "I don't know what your role, or your father's, is in this tragedy, but my family will take care of its own. Thank you for telling me about James. Good day." Without meeting her eyes, he stalked off toward his mother's house.

Something was wrong with Henry's story. Emily wasn't a lawyer, but she had grown up around the law. The story of the inheritance and the codicil seemed fishy. She wished her father were here to explain it.

But her father was still in Boston, and judging from Henry's hasty departure, she would get no answers from the Langstons. She would have to find a different way.

Death is like the insect

Menacing the tree,

Competent to kill it,

But decoyed may be

CHAPTER 15

Emily watched Henry as he disappeared on the College grounds. As though his departure were a signal for the heavens, the rain stopped.

"Well?" Vinnie said, stepping out from the shadows around the corner of the church. She was very damp.

"Oh!" Emily's hand flew to her mouth. "You gave me a start." She narrowed her eyes. "Did you follow me again?"

Vinnie nodded vigorously. "Henry Langston is rather handsome, but he's a suspicious character. I wasn't going to let you go alone."

Only a curmudgeon could resist Vinnie's devotion. Emily reached out and clasped her sister's hand. "You take better care of me than I deserve." She felt the stirrings of a cough deep in her chest, but she smothered it before it could be born. No need to worry Vinnie, who would be sure to tell their mother.

She noticed that Vinnie's cloth shoes were soaked and stained. She had refused to wear the practical boots that Emily's father had had made for them.

"But I'm perishing of curiosity—I couldn't hear a thing. What happened?" Vinnie asked.

"Mr. Nobody has a name," Emily said. "He's James Wentworth, Henry's cousin."

A slow smile appeared on Vinnie's face. "You thought he might be!"

Emily nodded sadly.

"But he was supposed to be dead already. How is it that he came back to Amherst to die again?"

"I'm more concerned about how he died in Amherst." Emily tucked a hand in Vinnie's elbow and led her toward home. "I wish Father had a criminal practice. Then we would be more knowledgeable about sudden death."

"Mother tells us enough stories out of the newspaper," Vinnie replied tartly. "What don't we know about grisly deaths?"

Emily laughed, grateful to her sister for leavening her mood. "Dr. Gridley suggested James Wentworth was poisoned, but he couldn't determine which poison."

"Can't he perform some sort of test, like they do in our chemistry lectures?" asked Vinnie.

"Only if he knows what poison to look for. I learned that in botany when we talked about antidotes."

They walked down South Pleasant Street, past the Common on their right. In the best of weather, the Common was a large soggy field, suitable only for hungry cows. Today it was a veritable frog pond. Emily could hear the tiny creatures croaking to one another, drowning out the persistent crickets. The Amherst House on the corner was doing good business, although the shops and offices were already closed for the evening. The gentle downward slope made the walk an easy one. They passed the widow Kellogg's house, with its tall hedge of yew.

Emily wrinkled her nose at the bitter smell of the trees. "Remember that little boy who died after he ate yew berries? Mother read it in the newspaper. The poison was called taxine."

"Who could forget?" Vinnie said with a smile. "Mother made us swear to avoid yew berries for the rest of our lives."

"It worries her how easy it would be for all of us to die. Killing a man is as easy as crushing berries from this tree and dropping it in his tea."

Vinnie stopped abruptly. "You think a yew berry killed your friend?"

"I don't know." Emily sighed. "There are so many ways to kill someone with ordinary plants." She paused, remembering her lessons. "And not everyone reacts to a plant toxin in the same way."

Miss Phelps had shown them how the brush of a tulip petal might irritate the skin. Ursula had shown no reaction, but Emily's skin had turned bright red and developed a rash. Miss Phelps said that meant she was "exquisitely sensitive," which was a botanist's term. Emily remembered how envious Ursula had been . . . of a rash! Apparently Ursula craved to be the center of all eyes. Again, Emily remembered how Ursula had worked tirelessly to make her herbarium outshine Emily's.

"I had no idea that plants were so dangerous. Let's hurry home," Vinnie said.

"Be grateful I don't tell you how toxic the forest is," Emily teased. But her steps quickened homeward as well.

Emily woke the next morning with the dreaded and familiar cough. She tried to hide it, but Vinnie propped herself up and began scolding. "Emily, you've been overdoing it. You should never have gone out in the rain yesterday."

"I'm fine. Stop coddling me." But Emily lay back on her pillow, her chest feeling hollowed-out and cold.

Vinnie slipped out of bed and put on her robe. "I was going on a picnic with Jane Gridley, but if you are ill, I'll stay home."

"Absolutely not!" Emily cried. "You go and enjoy yourself." She tried to keep the disappointment out of her voice. The picnic sounded fun, but Emily had not been invited. "I'll rest for a bit this morning, then I'll help Mother." She had planned to pursue her investigation today, but her duties at home took precedence.

"Well, if you insist, I'll go," Vinnie said. She looked as sly as one of her cats with cream dripping from its whiskers. "If you promise to rest, I'll bring you a clue when I get home."

"Have you been investigating on your own?" Emily accused.

With a secretive smile, Vinnie said, "I've just been doing exactly what I'm supposed to do . . . unlike another sister I could mention. Now sleep, or I won't tell you."

Emily rolled over and buried her head under the covers. No sooner had she begun to doze than she heard her mother enter the room. The only thing that could distract Mrs. Dickinson from her own ill-health was the prospect of nursing Emily.

Emily peeked out. "Good morning, Mother."

Her mother adjusted the blanket at Emily's feet, tucking it in at the corners of the bed. "Vinnie told me you're coughing. I sent for Dr. Gridley, but he's out of town until Sunday."

"That's not necessary. I feel fine now." Emily kicked the blanket loose.

"I thought you might like to speak to Dr. Gridley anyway—about your dead body," her mother continued, as though Emily hadn't spoken.

Startled, she glanced at her mother's pale face. There were shadows under her eyes, and Emily felt as guilty as if she had painted them there herself.

Her mother went on, "Isn't that what you've been sneaking out to do? Wouldn't it be more convenient if the doctor just came here?"

Emily wanted to pull the too-warm blanket over her head. She had underestimated her mother's powers of observation. "I found out the dead man's name," she admitted. "He can have a decent Christian burial now."

"That's admirable, I'm sure. But why was it so important to you?" Emily's mother sank down on the bed as though her legs wouldn't support her any longer.

Emily reached out and took her hand. "No one cared except me," she said.

"You aren't strong enough for such a crusade." Her mother's hand trembled in Emily's.

"If you keep me trapped in this house, I'll never get stronger," Emily retorted. At her mother's stricken look, she relented. "Besides, you and Father taught me to do the right thing."

Mrs. Dickinson's spine straightened and her chin lifted. "I've also tried to teach you how perilous the world is. Home is the only place you can be safe."

Emily felt as though she couldn't breathe, but it had nothing to do with her weak chest. "Safe—but suffocating."

"Suffocating?" Her mother pulled away from Emily's grasp and went to the window that faced the pond. Her back was rigid, and Emily knew she was remembering the corpse floating there.

Emily spoke to her mother's back. "I want to accomplish something with my life. I'll probably need to leave home sometimes, but I promise I'll always return . . . to find myself again."

"You are not meant to have adventures," Mrs. Dickinson snapped. "You're supposed to marry, have children of your own, and keep a beautiful house."

"What if I want something else?" Emily asked in a defiant voice. "Something that doesn't require a husband or children?"

"Of course you'll marry," Mrs. Dickinson said. "Lavinia will doubtless have more suitors, but there are many young men who will appreciate your intelligence, so long as you don't frighten them away with your odd ideas and your secret notebooks."

Emily's hand slid imperceptibly under her pillow, where she touched the reassuring square notebook filled with clues. It felt like a talisman.

Mrs. Dickinson came back to the bed and fluffed Emily's pillow around her head. "Vinnie is picnicking with that Jane Gridley. I'm not sure she's an appropriate friend for your sister; Jane is entirely too popular." She put a hand to her temple. "I'm feeling a headache coming on. I'm going to lie down. You should rest, too. Later, we'll do the baking."

"Yes, Mother."

"While you are lying here, think about what I've said. You are almost sixteen. It's time you understood the importance of doing your duty." She paused in the doorway. "And if you won't listen to me, I'm sure your father will be more persuasive." She closed the door.

"What could be more important than solving a murder?" Emily threw her pillow at the door.

If anybody's friend be dead
It's sharpest of the theme
The thinking how they walked alive,
At such and such a time.

CHAPTER 16

By that afternoon, Emily and her mother had reversed their roles.

"Emily!"

"Yes, Mama?"

"Close the curtains, please. The light is stabbing my eyes."

Emily hurried into the parlor carrying a tray bearing a glass of water and a bottle of Dr. Gridley's patented medicine for neuralgia.

"Hurry, Emily." Her mother lay on the softest sofa, her hand covering her eyes.

Emily pulled the curtains closed, trying not to let her gaze linger out the window. The brilliant August sunshine was a temptation she could not afford to indulge today.

She poured the medicine into the glass and offered it to her mother. "I don't know if I should take it," Mrs. Dickinson protested. "It always makes me so sleepy."

"Mama, it gives you relief." Emily gently raised the glass to her mother's lips. Mrs. Dickinson drank deeply, wincing at the sharp flavor of anise. "Sleep is a balm to your pain."

"But who will help you with the baking? There's so much to be done. I knew I shouldn't have let your sister go picnicking."

"Mama, Vinnie has been working so hard while I played truant that she deserves a treat. Dr. Gridley's daughter was kind to invite Vinnie to join the party." Emily concentrated to keep the envy out of her voice.

"But you've never done all the baking alone. . . . You aren't ready."

She laid her hand against her mother's cheek. "I was trained by the best housekeeper in Amherst. Think of this as my comprehensive exam."

"You'll remember to make several loaves of corn bread? And the coconut cake? I promised the Hitchcocks that I would bring some to the tea tomorrow . . ." The doctor's prescription began to take effect and Mrs. Dickinson drifted into sleep.

Emily stared down at her mother, wrestling with a mixture of irritation and affection. With a shrug, she trudged into the kitchen. Half a dozen pans were out, waiting for batter and baking. She brought out the milk and eggs from the icebox. She compared the number of the eggs with her baking requirements. There wouldn't be enough.

Slipping wooden clogs over her indoor slippers, she went out to the chicken coop, leaving the kitchen door wide open in the hope that a summer's breeze might blow out the stifling heat from the oven.

When she returned to the kitchen, a basket of eggs on her arm, she stopped short.

Henry Wentworth was leaning against the battered table in the center of the kitchen. He wore a casual suit, and his wide grin suggested he was confident of his welcome.

"Henry! What are you doing here?" she asked, tucking a stray strand of hair behind her ear.

"I was coming to invite you for a ride and I spied you heading to the coop. I'm afraid of chickens, so I thought I would wait inside." His eyes sparkled, as though he were asking her to laugh at him. "I hope you don't mind?"

Grasping the basket tighter, Emily's thoughts were racing. When she had seen him last, he had been grief-stricken.

Although she had found his tears plausible, she still harbored suspicions that Henry knew more than he'd told her. And now he was acting as though he hadn't a care in the world.

Slowly her feet brought her inside the kitchen, but she left the door propped open. Not meeting his eyes, she untied her filthy apron, stained with the juice of bushels of strawberries from this year's jam-making. She took Vinnie's much cleaner apron off the peg and fastened it around her neck.

"Of course I don't mind," she finally managed to say. "Won't you sit down? Can I get you something to drink? Cold water?" She deposited the basket on the edge of the table without her usual care. It began to tip.

"Careful!" Henry caught the basket, rescuing the eggs, and placed it in the center of the table.

"Thank you," Emily said, her pulse racing as though it were her own body that had nearly crashed to the ground. She was acutely aware that she was alone with him, and that her mother wouldn't wake up if an earthquake shook the rafters.

"Now that I've done my good deed for the day, I'll have that water." Henry pulled his tie loose and wiped the perspiration from his brow.

Emily's hand flew to her mouth. Mr. Nobody had used that same gesture in the smithy. For a moment it was as if Henry was gone and Mr. Nobody had taken his place.

"Emily? You did offer me water, didn't you?"

"What?" Emily regretfully returned to the present. "Of course." She pumped water at the sink into a pitcher and poured a glass for him.

Henry drank deeply. "Miss Dickinson, would you like to go for a drive and enjoy this beautiful day?"

Emily's gaze went to the rolling hills outside the window, freshly scrubbed after yesterday's rain. The apples on the trees in the orchard shone, and even the gravestones in the cemetery glistened. The freshness out of doors made the kitchen even more stifling.

He continued, "It would be a kindness to help me take my mind from our family's loss."

Emily jerked her attention back to his face, trying to see the truth in his features. Was James's death the family's loss or gain? Surely Henry, as charming as he seemed, profited from his cousin's demise? She might never have another opportunity to find out. What harm could an excursion hold?

But then she looked back at the kitchen table and the never-ending baking. "I'm afraid I can't," she said.

Henry glanced around at all the pans. "How much do you have to bake? You look as though you were making enough to feed all of Amherst!"

"Four loaves of cornbread, three loaves of bread, a coconut cake, and a chicken pie for dinner tonight." Emily counted on her fingers. "Actually, it's a capon pie. Austin's rooster finally disturbed my mother's sleep one too many times." She gestured to the carcass by the sink, feathers already plucked.

"Who killed the rooster?" Henry asked, staring at Emily as though she had sprouted a second head.

"I did, of course. Vinnie is too soft-hearted."

"That is unexpectedly ruthless of you," he said.

"Not terribly. Mother insists that we be as sufficient unto ourselves as we can. But this particular rooster's sacrifice will be a blow to Austin. I don't know how I'll break the news to him."

"And who is Austin?" Henry asked.

"My older brother. He's away at school. I miss him terribly."

He nodded. "When I'm away, I miss my sister. More than I appreciate her when I'm home!"

"Are you and Ursula close?" she asked.

"Close enough," he said. "I'm the eldest by five years and our parents aren't very practical, so I've always felt responsible for her."

"Austin tries to take care of me. Vinnie, too, despite that I am the elder. Without them, I would be lost." Her hands were busy measuring the flour into a large mixing bowl. "But if I'm to be completely honest—I wouldn't mind losing my way sometimes. One never knows what one will see."

"I like the way you phrase things, Emily."

Emily laughed, and she began to relax. After all, hadn't she deduced that Henry was genuinely shocked when he saw his cousin's body? Whatever mystery swirled around James's death, Henry's part could not be so nefarious. After all, she and Henry had shed tears together.

Henry went on. "Tell me what I can do to help. If I can't tempt you outside, the least I can do is assist with the baking."

Emily shook her head with a smile. "I can't see you cooking. Your clothes are too fine."

"That can be remedied," he replied, removing his suit coat and hanging it over a chair. He rolled up the sleeves of his linen shirt. Emily noticed his thin wrists and long fingers. She remembered the strength of James's hands as he had lifted her off the stable floor. She wanted to reach out and touch Henry's hands, but stopped herself. What was she thinking? Despite their resemblance, Henry was not his cousin.

Emily turned away, feeling a flush moving up her neck to her face. She pushed two eggs toward him. "Very well. I need these cracked into this bowl for the coconut cake."

"That sounds easy enough." He grabbed an egg and squeezed it into his fist over the bowl. Emily began to giggle as he turned his hand over, letting the sticky mess drip into the bowl. She handed him a clean cloth.

"There's a trick—I'll show you. But first let me rescue that egg," she said. "Mama always says, 'Waste not want not.'" She picked the white bits of shell out of the golden yolk. "Like snowflakes in summer," she murmured.

"I beg your pardon?" Henry asked.

Her clean hand reached for the hidden compartment in her corset for her notebook until she remembered Henry's presence. She glanced about the kitchen and spied Jasper's shoeing bill from the smithy. She took her silver pencil from around her neck and scribbled on the paper. The words secure for later use, she replaced the pencil around her neck. She looked up to see Henry staring at her.

"I'm sorry," she said. "I needed to write something down."

"May I see?"

"No!" She caught herself. "I don't show anyone my words."

"Words?" He raised his blond eyebrows. "So Miss Emily Dickinson considers herself a writer?"

What was the mysterious power these cousins had? No one outside her family knew her secret—but James and now Henry had discovered it in no time at all.

Hurriedly, she changed the subject. "Can you check my recipe for the amount of cream of tartar?"

With a small grin, he picked up the piece of paper. "One teaspoon cream of tartar." His eyes, dancing with mischief, rested on her face. Could he see the blood rushing to shame her expression? "Will you write about me later, Miss Emily?"

"Absolutely not," she said. "Why on earth would I write about you?" Here was a difference between the cousins. When James had discovered she wrote, he had talked about Emily. Henry spoke of himself.

"I'm an intriguing character," he teased.

She picked up a wooden spoon and shook it in his direction as though she were brandishing a sword. "I'm not interested in intriguing characters."

"Then what does interest you?"

"My impressions of what I see around me. My own thoughts." Too late, she realized how immodest that might sound.

"I'm sure your thoughts are a fascinating study," he said, a mocking gleam in his eyes.

Catching her lower lip between her teeth, she pointed to the recipe in Henry's hand. "And the soda? How much?"

"One half teaspoon." He turned the page over. "Where are the instructions? Shouldn't a recipe tell you what to do?"

"Not mine." She flashed him a quick grin. "I like lists of ingredients. Then I decide what to do with them."

"To what end?"

"Chemical combustion!"

"The way your eyes glisten quite frightens me," Henry said. "What does an Amherst miss know of combustion?"

"Quite a lot," Emily assured him. "We take chemistry lectures at the College. Hasn't Ursula told you?"

He spread out his hands. "If it doesn't involve fashion or botany, Ursula is a closed book."

"All her clothes are lovely, and she's very clever in botany," Emily conceded, stirring in the tartar. Henry took a seat at the table and watched her, his chin resting on the bridge of his interlaced hands. "And now the soda."

"The ladies in my family wouldn't have the first idea how to make a coconut cake, much less kill a capon. That's a job for the servants." he said idly. He sat up straight. "I beg your pardon, Emily. That sounded snobbish. You've met my mother—I would hate to sound as pretentious as she."

"Not at all," Emily said. "We Dickinsons are true to our Puritan forebears—don't pay anyone to do what you can do yourself! But that doesn't mean everyone else has to be a slave to our principles."

She added a cup each of coconut and sugar to the bowl and then two cups of flour.

"My mother believes in the domestic arts," Emily confided, glancing guiltily at the door to the parlor, "but I would happily trade my baking duties for a pencil and paper and a quiet desk."

"And what will you write? Gothic romances? Chemical treatises? Poetry?" He caught sight of her expression. "Ah, a poet in the making."

Emily's mood turned wistful. "Your cousin managed to get me to admit that, too. You two must have been quite the pair."

Henry stared out the window. His clouded face was in sharp contrast to the clear summer sky. "We were indeed. We only saw each other at school holidays, and away from Mother. She didn't approve of James or his father. But we had plenty of adventures."

Emily felt a guilty pang that it was so easy to talk with Henry. Had she forgotten James so quickly? But she couldn't resist hearing stories about him. "Tell me," she prompted as she stirred.

"Once we climbed Mount Washington in New Hampshire. We were caught by a freak snowstorm in October. We almost died." A reminiscent smile played on his lips. "Those were excellent times."

Emily shook her head. "An excellent time? Almost dying? It amazes me what young men find 'excellent.'"

"Even the almost dying was fun—because of course we didn't! But James and I liked pushing ourselves." His eyes took on a sad cast, perhaps remembering that his cousin would never again rise to the challenge. "Whenever we visited Uncle, we used to race each other across the Connecticut River—the faster flowing it was, the more we liked it."

Folding over the batter and working in the thick

coconut, Emily rolled her eyes. "The river isn't safe—it's a wonder you weren't drowned."

He shrugged. "The danger was the fun part."

"Sometimes I could scream at how little adventure I am allowed to enjoy," Emily said. "But do tell me more. If I cannot have adventures, it gives me pleasure to hear of other people's."

"Well, I remember the time we camped in Rattlesnake Gulch. We swore we would bring home a rattlesnake!"

Pouring the cake batter into the pans, Emily asked, "And did you?"

He looked rueful. "No. We saw a bear and came running home. After that we stayed closer to Uncle's house, exploring the Indian trails." He sighed. "I miss those days. I wish James wasn't dead."

There was silence, finally broken by Emily. "The batter is ready," she said. She crossed over to the oven, opened the door, and stuck her hand in. Henry stared while she counted.

"One, two, three, four . . . " When she got to ten, the heat was unbearable and she snatched her hand away. "The oven is ready," she said.

"Emily!" Henry grabbed her forearm to examine the redness on her hand. Without releasing her, he poured water from the pitcher onto a cloth and carefully wrapped her hand. "I had no idea that baking was so dangerous!"

"All domestic duties are hazardous to your health," Emily retorted. "One is apt to die of boredom! I'd rather have rattlesnakes and bears any day."

Henry laughed loudly. Emily hushed him, but it was too late.

"Emily!" Mrs. Dickinson's querulous voice could be heard from the parlor. "Who's here? Did I hear someone?"

"I'll be right there, Mama," Emily called.

Henry stood up. "I had better be going and leave you to your alarming household chores."

"I would rather have gone for a ride with you," Emily said, shocked at how easily the sentiment slipped from her lips.

"Another time," Henry said, pleased. With a slight bow, he took his leave.

Emily turned on her heel toward the parlor. Her hand was on the doorknob when a thought suddenly occurred to her. Henry had told her that he and James were strong enough swimmers to race the swift-moving Connecticut River. Then why had he been so willing to believe that James had drowned? Was she the only person who saw the questions surrounding his death?

"Emily!" Her mother's voice was full of her drugged sleep.

Emily put aside her suspicions for later consideration. Summoning a suitably cheerful tone, she called out, "Coming, Mother."

Until they lock it in the grave,

'Tis bliss I cannot weigh

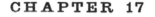

CHAPTER 17

The next morning Emily was ready to return to her investigation as soon as the breakfast dishes were cleared from the table. Her mother was gone, Emily's coconut cake in hand, to spend the day with Mrs. Hitchcock. Emily tried to leave quietly by the front door, only to find Vinnie blocking her way.

"You're staying inside, Emily Elizabeth," Vinnie said. "We can talk about the case here."

"We can talk, but then I'm going out. Alone," Emily said. She sank down on a sofa, trying to quell a cough in her chest.

"Only if I decide you are well enough to go," Vinnie said firmly.

Knowing she was defeated for the moment, Emily took a deep breath and began. "James's death was meant to look like an accidental drowning, but he had no water in his lungs. And someone dressed his body in Horace Goodman's clothes and deposited it in our pond."

Vinnie said, "Was it Henry Langston?"

"Henry? I don't think he's a killer," Emily said.

Vinnie shot her sister a penetrating look. "You call him Henry now?"

Blushing, Emily said, "Never mind."

"Do you think you have let Henry's charm keep you from looking at the facts with a clear head?" Vinnie asked, collapsing next to her on the sofa.

"Of course not," Emily insisted. "I can be completely disinterested."

"Prove it!"

"I can't deny there's a strong case against Henry," Emily admitted. "Who else knew James was alive?" She started counting on her fingers. "One, he admitted meeting his cousin the day before he died. Two, Henry drives the carriage that probably brought James to the pond. It's his uncle's carriage; remember Sam Wentworth wasn't home the day James stopped by the farm, because he was buying the carriage."

"Go on," Vinnie said.

"Third, Henry certainly had motive enough to want James dead; his family's fortunes depended upon it."

"Very damning," Vinnie said in a thrilled whisper.

"And we know Henry is a liar," Emily pointed out. "He told his mother that he just arrived, but he's been here for several days."

"What if there's an innocent explanation?" Vinnie asked.

Emily raised her eyebrows.

With a mischievous grin, Vinnie asked, "If your mother were Violet Langston, wouldn't you want to avoid spending time with her?"

They giggled. Then Vinnie, sobered, said, "But if Henry lies so well to his family, how can we depend on anything he says?"

"We can't," Emily said decisively. "But let's look at the case for his innocence. Henry was genuinely upset when he saw his cousin's body. Unless he is a marvelous actor, I would swear he didn't know James was dead until that moment."

"A point in his favor," Vinnie agreed.

"And there are logical reasons to believe his innocence as well. How did he get Horace Goodman's clothes to dress the body? Henry is a law student who lives in New Haven. Would he even know the family's handyman, much less trust him to disguise a corpse?"

"That's an excellent point," Vinnie agreed.

"Unless he had an accomplice," Emily said. "Anyone in his family had the same motive."

"That does make it more difficult," Vinnie said.

The silence in the room offered proof of the hard thinking going on.

"Emily, this is making me a little worried about Father."

Emily gave her sister a puzzled look. "Why?"

"That codicil you found said James was dead. His own father said so, yes?"

"I have serious doubts that Jeremiah Wentworth knew anything about that codicil. He was in the Dakotas at the time," Emily said.

"Maybe, but the point is that the codicil was filed in Father's office!" Vinnie's voice was trembling, as though she were on the brink of deducing something awful. "Could he be blamed?"

"We could lose everything," Emily whispered. Their grandfather's improvidence had driven the Dickinsons perilously close to bankruptcy. The specter of poverty always hovered over the household. Emily sometimes had terrifying dreams where she and her mother were forced to earn a backbreaking living growing rye in the fields.

"It would kill Mother," Vinnie said.

Emily thought it through. "Father wrote Jeremiah's first will years ago. The codicil was added only last November when Father was in Washington. Mr. Ripley wrote and witnessed that codicil." She smothered a cough. "I think the Langstons took advantage of Father's absence to bribe Mr. Ripley. He wrote the codicil that guaranteed the Langstons a fortune, and now Mr. Ripley is suspiciously well off."

"You think so?" asked Vinnie, worry still in her voice.

"Stop fretting." Emily embraced her sister. "Father isn't in any danger, but I do think a conversation with Mr. Ripley might be useful."

"There's another way to find out what Mr. Ripley knows." Vinnie jumped up and ran out of the room, returning a moment later. She handed her sister a folded square of paper.

"What's this?" Emily said, unfolding it.

"Do you steal so much used blotting paper that you can't remember this one?"

"I thought I lost this!" Emily said. "I took it from Mr. Ripley's desk while someone was accusing me of being a lunatic."

"I found it in your skirt pocket when I was tidying up." Vinnie stared at the ceiling with a cherubic air. "You see the value to housework? You should try it yourself."

"Shall we see what it says?" Emily flattened the paper. A scattering of words in reverse was spread across it. "We'll need a mirror."

They went into the hall and held up the blotting paper to the reflection. "Here are the words 'Wentworth' and 'Langston.' And what is that word?" Vinnie asked.

Emily tried to decipher the cramped handwriting. "I think it says 'confession' and 'fraud.' And 'sworn affidavit.'"

"How suspicious is it that Mr. Ripley was writing such words about the Wentworths?" Vinnie asked.

"Maybe James Wentworth forced Mr. Ripley to write a confession of what he had done?" Emily suggested. "Maybe Mr. Ripley killed him to get it back? Or perhaps James confronted the Langstons with the proof?"

Vinnie leaned against the wall and sighed. "What a club to use against them all." Her face twisted. "Emily, what happens to the Langstons now? Will they lose all the money? What will become of Ursula?"

"I don't know," Emily admitted. "If James had been dead all along as they claimed, then the Langstons would inherit anyway. But if they killed him, the law doesn't permit them to profit from their crime."

A glimpse of Mr. Nobody waving cheerfully as he disappeared into the rain filled her thoughts. Within the privacy of her mind, he would always be Mr. Nobody. "If they killed James, they should be punished."

"You sound so determined, Emily," Vinnie said. "You are quite frightening."

A loud knock at the door made them both flinch. Emily and Vinnie exchanged glances, uncomfortably aware that they were alone in the house.

"Who is it?" Vinnie asked in a whisper.

"Can I see through doors?" Emily retorted. She tiptoed to the door and peeked through the side window. "It's all right," she said in relief and swung open the door.

Reverend Colton filled the doorframe. He beamed when he saw them. "Good afternoon, girls. Is your mother at home?"

Emily invited him in. "She's visiting with friends today. May I give her a message?"

The reverend looked thoughtful. "I just came to tell her that the funeral for young Wentworth, the gentleman found in your pond, will be tomorrow."

"But he was only identified the day before yesterday." Emily's voice squawked.

He nodded. "The family wants a quick burial—and as you know, there are reasons that will be desirable."

Emily and Vinnie, veterans of many vigils for the dead in warm weather, nodded ruefully.

"But what about Dr. Gridley?" Emily asked.

The reverend raised his eyebrows, a pair of gray tufted question marks above his brown eyes.

"Doesn't the doctor have to decide on a cause of death?" Emily asked. Unable to stay seated, she began to pace about the room.

"Emily, he drowned." Reverend Colton's eyes followed her progress back and forth. "My sexton pulled him out of your pond."

"But . . ." Emily stopped, realizing that to go further would involve her in far too many explanations. How could she tell Reverend Colton that if James's body were six feet under, it would be too late to test for poison?

"The family wants the utmost discretion." He looked uncomfortable.

Emily stopped and faced him. "Then why are you telling us?" she asked. Vinnie shot her a scandalized look.

The reverend's face reflected a battle between tact and curiosity. "I thought it was the least I could do for your mother." He paused. "I'm not well acquainted with the Langstons. Do you know them well?" he asked almost too casually. Emily had the distinct impression that his burning curiosity about the family was the true reason for his visit.

"I went to school with Ursula for one term, and of course we've met them at social functions in town," Emily explained.

"But they don't have anything to do with the College, so our circles don't mix very often," Vinnie added.

"Well, the funeral is the family's responsibility and the arrangements are for them to decide." He glanced at Vinnie. "Lavinia, I'm quite thirsty. May I trouble you for a glass of water?"

"Of course, reverend." Her face flushed scarlet. "I am so sorry that I didn't offer before." She almost ran to the kitchen.

Reverend Colton turned to Emily and said, "How are you feeling, my dear?"

"My cough is almost completely gone," Emily said warily.

"I don't mean physically." After a silence Emily was reluctant to break, he went on. "The last time I saw you, you were upset. Are you calmer now that the investigation is done?"

Emily nearly choked. "My investigation?"

"Emily, your activities have been noticed and commented upon. Since I originally encouraged you, I've done my best to choke off any gossip. But you know that's like trying to hold back the tide in this town. "

So that was how Emily's mother knew of her interest in the dead body. Emily traced the intricate pattern in her mother's brocade with her finger. "I would so much rather be anonymous. It's dreary to be somebody. One doesn't have any privacy at all."

The reverend's smile appeared and disappeared so rapidly that Emily thought she might have imagined it. "Without you," he said, "James Wentworth might never have been identified. Well done. But your part is finished."

"But no one knows what happened to him . . . "

"That's a question for the authorities. Be content that tomorrow he's being buried under his own proper name. I am in deadly earnest, young lady. You must stop." He looked at Emily and sighed at her obstinacy. "Your mother . . . "

"My mother wants me to waste my life baking and preserving. Her house is too tidy to allow for justice."

Reverend Colton laid his hand on Emily's. "Justice?" he asked gently. "Is that your only concern here?"

Emily squirmed under his penetrating gaze. "What other concern could I have?" she asked. Did he know that the law offices of Edward Dickinson might be involved in a fraud?

"He was a very handsome young man," he said. "Not much older than you are."

Emily felt the heat spreading across her face. "Reverend Colton, that's not it at all!" She shook her head violently. "Tell me, what should I do if suspect that something terrible has been done? A mortal sin?"

"Let the authorities do their duty, my dear."

"The authorities don't care!"

The reverend looked thoughtful. "If you persist, your reputation may suffer."

"What is my reputation compared to finding the truth for James Wentworth?" Emily cried.

He glanced toward the kitchen. "Emily, may I be blunt?"

"Please!"

His hint of a smile was replaced by a somberness that frightened her. "You are suggesting that James Wentworth was murdered?"

"Perhaps," Emily said warily.

"And yet you plan to keep investigating? Despite the danger to yourself?"

"How could I be in any danger?" Emily said.

"Don't you think a killer is dangerous?"

"I don't have anything a killer would want," Emily said uncertainly.

"You represent a threat to his safety. If someone has once seen a solution to his problem in murder, he may kill again to protect himself." He shook his head sadly. "It gets easier."

Emily felt a chill in her chest that had nothing to do with her cough. "What a terrible thought."

Before the reverend could respond, Vinnie returned with a glass of water and a plate of gingerbread. He enjoyed the piece of cake and then drained his glass.

Reverend Colton stood up to take his leave. "What time is the funeral tomorrow?" Emily asked. "We don't want to be late."

He raised his eyebrows in an exasperated movement. "I beg your pardon?"

"Of course my family must be represented," Emily said. "The body was found here."

"The Langston family has particularly asked for a private ceremony."

"Oh," said Emily.

The reverend patted her shoulder. "Remember what I said. Good afternoon." The door closed behind him. Vinnie shot her sister a concerned look and sighed at the rebellion she saw on Emily's face.

"You can't go to the funeral," Vinnie warned. "Mother would have a fit."

"Perhaps not," Emily said. "But I can watch. What's the point of living next to the cemetery if we can't enjoy the funerals?"

If nature will not tell the tale

Jehovah told to her,

Can human nature not survive

Without a listener?

CHAPTER 18

Later that day, Emily clambered on top of the field-stone wall that marked the far end of their garden. She glanced back, just able to make out Vinnie in a pale yellow dress picking herbs in the garden. Vinnie, with an instinct that Emily found exasperating, looked toward Emily's perch. Emily froze until her sister's attention returned to the sage and rosemary.

"I'm sorry, but if Reverend Colton is right, I must investigate on my own," she murmured. It wasn't fair to put Vinnie in danger.

Reviewing the clues, she had realized that she had neglected to visit Amethyst Brook, where the Indian pipes grew. Somehow the unusual plant had found its way into James's collar; he must have been there. That morning Emily had looked up her father's map of Amherst to find the spot.

At a brisk pace, she cut through to Triangle Street, going down one side of the geometrical street and then the other. Within minutes she had emerged on the road to Pelham. Today the crows were missing, which she saw as a good omen. She passed Sam Wentworth's house, behind its orchards roiling with bees. She hurried by and found the path to the brook between two fields on the left side of the dirt road. She hadn't realized that his house was so close to her destination.

A farmer had cultivated corn in the twin fields; the stalks towered above her head. This farmer had a taste of whimsy, for he had planted sunflowers at the end of the field. She imagined their faces were turned toward her, bobbing with gentle courtesy.

Suddenly the open fields were gone and she was in the woods. She heard the rippling of water over rocks before she saw the brook. It was about twenty-five feet across, and the water had worn away the ground underneath the trees on the banks so they seemed to levitate above the water. The forest on either side was a thousand shades of green and allowed dappled sunlight to reach the pine needles thick on the ground. She inhaled deeply, reveling in a tranquility disturbed only by the chirping of small birds. She would wager that no matter what happened here, joy or despair, this river would always look the same.

She pulled out her notebook and licked the end of her silver pencil.

After a hundred years
Nobody knows the place,—
Agony, that enacted there,
Motionless as peace.

She crossed out a few words and tried jotting a few other choices. She waited, but nothing more came to her. She carefully tucked the notebook back in its hiding place and began searching for the ghostly pale petals and wooden stems of an Indian pipe. She found a stand almost immediately next to a half-rotted log. In the bright afternoon, the eerie plant looked almost ordinary.

"All right, I've found the flower that isn't a flower. Can I prove that James was indeed here?" Emily began searching, lifting dead branches and pushing aside foliage. Before long she noticed an area where the pine needles were scuffed, as though some violent disturbance had taken place. A glint of gold where no gold should be caught her eye. She brushed aside a patch of feathery ferns to find a gold watch with the monogram "W."

"Proof," Emily said aloud.

"Proof of what?"

She whirled around, shoving the watch into her skirt pocket. Henry leaned against a tree not five paces away. How had he come up behind her so silently? His face was in shadow, and she couldn't see his eyes. He seemed an altogether different person than the charming suitor who had helped her with the baking.

"Nothing," she said. "Did you follow me here?"

He hesitated, his lips pressed tightly together. Finally he said, "We saw you walk by Uncle's house. I wondered if you were still meddling in our family's affairs."

She took a step backward. "And if I am?"

"Everyone is satisfied with my cousin's death . . . except you."

Emily's heart beat faster as she realized how far she was from home and help. "I must be going now," she said and tried to move past him. Henry suddenly grabbed her wrist.

"Let me go," she said, struggling to keep her voice level. His hand remained, and she repeated in a higher voice, "Let me go! Henry, my family knows that I am here."

"First you have to listen to me," he said. "I seem to recall you made a similar bargain with me."

MICHAELA MACCOLL

His genial voice belied the threat she heard only too clearly. Emily pressed her knees together, as though that could stop the trembling of her whole body. "I'm listening."

His fingers still tight around her wrist, he called into the woods. "Uncle, come out."

A twig cracked, and Sam Wentworth emerged from behind a stand of trees. Emily tugged futilely at Henry's grip. Two men with a secret—and no help within earshot. And Reverend Colton had warned her that very morning!

"Good morning, Miss Dickinson," Sam said slowly. He was still frightening, but Emily noticed that his eyes were bloodshot and his skin looked mottled. He looked like someone who had suffered a great loss. "I'd like to apologize for the way I treated you the other day."

Emily said nothing.

"You are angry," he said. "I can't blame you. It was unforgivable."

"He's been under a great deal of strain," Henry said.

"Is that any excuse for threatening me, an innocent passerby?" Emily countered.

"Innocent! You were trespassing. And stealing. And asking impertinent questions!" Sam almost shouted.

"This is how you apologize?" Emily asked, glaring at Sam.

"Uncle!" Henry said warningly. "We're trying to make things right." He stood close behind her, his arm pressing against her body.

Emily lifted her chin and asked, "Why did you follow me here?"

"First, tell me how you found this place, girl," Sam said in a more measured tone. But Emily saw that his eyes still had a wild look.

"Let me go," she said. Henry glanced at his uncle and released her wrist. She rubbed the soreness.

"A flower led me here." Emily's voice quavered. She cleared her throat and went on more forcefully, "James died here, didn't he?" They stared at her as though they had seen a ghost. "Don't bother to deny it. I already know almost everything." A sense of prudence suggested she add, "And my father, the attorney, knows everything, too." How she wished that were true.

Sam stared at her, and the tension filling his body seemed to unwind like a spool of thread. He sank down on the rotting log and wiped his brow. "Last Sunday, I went to visit my sister. As I arrived, I met my nephew James on his way out of their garden. I couldn't believe that he was alive. I was so glad to see him."

"What did he say?" Emily asked, fascinated to learn the details of James's last day.

Sam stared at her with empty eyes. "He was in a temper. Someone had struck him in the face—I could see the mark. He brushed me aside. He said I was as criminal as the rest of the family. My sister Violet and her husband, Charles, were standing in the door watching us."

"Was anyone else there?" Emily asked.

"Just Ursula, watching from the window. I could see she had been crying," Sam said. "I went after James. I didn't want him to think he had been cheated."

"Especially by his own flesh and blood," Emily said.

Sam winced as though Emily had struck him, but he continued. "James walked away, furious. I was hard put to keep up with him. At first I thought he was coming to my house, but he passed it by and came here."

"How did he even know about Amethyst Brook?" Emily asked. "I've been walking around Amherst my whole life and I've never been here."

"I showed him," Henry said unexpectedly. "Do you remember how I told you that when we were boys, we visited our uncle? We explored all these old trails. This was a favorite spot."

"I finally caught him up here," Sam said. "I admitted what we had done." His voice stumbled, as though he couldn't bear to say it.

Henry rested his hand on his uncle's shoulder.

"The Langstons faked James's death so they could inherit your brother's fortune," Emily said impatiently. "I know that. But what happened next?"

"How do you know all this?" Henry spluttered.

"James said he had more than enough proof to prosecute the whole family for fraud," Sam continued.

"He would have had a good case, too," said Henry, ever the law student.

Emily considered that. Sam would go to jail, and possibly Mr. and Mrs. Langston would too. Henry, even if he wasn't involved, would be ruined. Who would hire a lawyer whose parents were in jail for fraud? And Ursula would be left penniless, for all intents and purposes an orphan.

"I told James that I hadn't known that he was still alive," Sam said. "His eyes seemed to stare through me, into my soul."

Emily's skin prickled—she knew that gaze.

"Finally he said, 'I believe you, Uncle.' He also said he didn't want to prosecute."

Emily frowned. "You expect me to believe that?"

"Yes!" Sam cried. "James said he wanted to try his hand at prospecting in California. The family could set him up handsomely and he wouldn't trouble them again."

Emily saw the doubt written across Henry's face and knew it was mirrored on her own. "Then what happened?" Emily asked, although she knew how this had to end. Somehow James's dead body had been dressed in new clothes, a telltale Indian pipe fortuitously trapped in his borrowed collar to lead her to this place.

"James laughed," Sam said.

"What?" Emily exclaimed. "I don't believe it."

"As surely as my bees love clover," Sam said. "He sat on this very spot and laughed. He said his Aunt Violet had always scolded him for being a ne'er-do-well. And now she had committed a crime and stolen a fortune. It was a great joke to him."

Emily was torn. On the one hand, it sounded exactly like the young man she had so briefly known. On the other hand, Sam Wentworth's tale was convenient. If it was true, then he had no reason to kill his nephew.

Sam saw her indecision and became agitated. "I'm telling the truth! He even gave me his proof." He pulled out a sheet of paper that matched the blotter Emily had stolen. "You will never guess what this is."

"An affidavit from a law clerk named Mr. Ripley, admitting he forged a codicil to Jeremiah's will?" Emily asked.

"You are a witch," said Henry, stunned. "How do you know all of my family's secrets?"

Emily shrugged, not taking her eyes from Sam. "Why did he give you that document? Why not use it to get his fortune back?"

"I told you—he said he wouldn't prosecute. Giving it to me was his sign of good faith."

"Or you took it from him after he was dead," Emily said.

"That's a lie!" Sam roused himself enough to protest. "Besides, Ripley is a coward. By all accounts, he would happily confess again. I'd have gained nothing from killing James. He gave me the affidavit."

Steeling her courage, Emily said in a stern voice, "Give it to me."

Sam hesitated. "I'm not going to give you proof that I've committed a crime!"

Emily went on, "My father is the attorney who wrote your brother's first will. The affidavit comes from his office. Besides, you said yourself that Mr. Ripley would tell anyone who asked."

Henry leaned over and whispered in his uncle's ear. Sam thought for a few moments, then handed it over.

Emily scanned the document, her eyebrows raising higher and higher. "Why didn't he give it to the Langstons?"

A wry smile appeared on Sam's lips. "He was enjoying their consternation."

Henry grinned. "He always had a wicked sense of humor."

"He's not the wicked one here, Henry," Emily snapped. "Mr. Wentworth, your story is missing an ending. How did Mr. No—James die?"

Sam lifted his shoulders. "I don't know. He pulled out a flask and we drank to his miraculous resurrection."

Emily nodded; she remembered that flask.

"A few minutes later, he clutched his chest and began to stagger about."

"He was poisoned!" Emily cried.

"No, he couldn't have been. I drank some of the wine first," Sam protested.

"Wine?" Emily leapt on the word. "Are you sure it wasn't brandy?"

He nodded. "I'm sure. I took a healthy swallow. It was elderberry wine. If it was poison, why wasn't I affected?"

"Did he say anything before . . . he died?" Emily's voice was rough. She saw Henry wince, and remembered that the cousins had once been close.

"He shouted that I was turning green. Then he fell down dead." Sam choked up and couldn't speak.

"There's more," Emily contradicted him. "Mr. Wentworth, you saw James was beyond help, so you went to your sister and brother-in-law."

"Violet and Charles were overjoyed." His mouth twisted at the memory. "My own sister . . ."

Emily glanced at Henry, wondering how he felt hearing such terrible things about his parents. He met her gaze with a blank look before he turned away.

Sam began to choke up. "Their own nephew was dead, and all they could think of was money."

Emily went on, "So they sent their hired man, Horace, to help you."

Surprisingly, Sam shook his head. "Horace used to work for me years ago. He'd do anything for me." He hesitated, with a sidelong glance at Henry. "Charles and Violet came up with a plan. No one in town was likely to remember James as my nephew—even I barely recognized him. We thought if we changed his appearance he could never be connected to us."

"You used Horace's clothes," Emily said. "And Horace carried the body to the road and put him into your new carriage."

Sam stared at her, dumbfounded. "Yes, God forgive me. We took him to the pond near the West Cemetery and slid him into the water."

"Why did you pick that pond?" Emily asked.

Sam shrugged. "It was on the road out of town, and no one in our family has any ties there."

"So it was merely a coincidence?" Emily said.

He nodded.

"You hoped he would be mistaken for a tramp who fell and drowned," Henry said.

"Yes," Sam said simply.

"If it weren't for Emily, your plan would have worked," Henry said. Emily thought he sounded almost regretful.

"A vile plan," Emily cried. "How could you let your own nephew be buried in a potter's field, unmarked and forgotten?"

"Charles said he would make an anonymous donation for a funeral." Sam rubbed at his eyes with his dirty palms. "But I don't think he did."

"You are a foolish old man," Emily said.

"I know," Sam said, pushing himself off the log. Henry moved to assist him, but Sam shook him off. Without saying another word, the old man lumbered off toward home, bits of rotten wood falling from his pants like a trail of breadcrumbs in the forest.

"Well, Emily," Henry said, very formally, "on behalf of my cousin James, I suppose I must thank you. Because of you, he will have the funeral he deserves." He took her hands in his.

Emily stared down at his soft hands that had never known a day's hard labor. She remembered the calluses on James's hands, and how they had marked him as a man who worked for his living. Not a thief. Nor someone who was willing to profit from theft. Slowly she pulled her hands away, and once and for all she stepped back from Henry Langston.

"Nothing is finished," she said in a low voice. "We still don't know how he died."

"You heard Uncle," Henry protested. "He fell down dead. James died of natural causes."

"He was murdered," Emily said. There. The words were spoken and could not be taken back.

"How?" Henry asked. "Uncle drank from the same flask. Emily, I'm grateful for your help, but I can handle things from here. I'll confront my parents."

"And the money?" Emily asked. "What will you do about the money?"

"With James's death, it comes to them anyway," he said. "No harm has been done."

"No harm?" Emily said in disgust. "The apple never falls far from the tree, and its seeds are the next generation of villainy. Your parents violated every rule of decency and betrayed every family tie. Could it be more foul?" She sank to the grass. Tears welled in her eyes as she thought of clever, gallant James. He was worth ten of Henry. He deserved the truth. No matter who got hurt.

"Emily, I'm warning you—it's finished. James will be buried properly, and the Langstons shall leave Amherst forever. That should satisfy you." He stalked off in the same direction as his uncle.

Staring after him, Emily whispered, "You haven't given up all your secrets yet, Henry. Until I find out everything, I won't be satisfied at all."

I Felt a funeral, in my brain,

And mourners, to and fro

Kept treading, treading, till it seemed

That sense was breaking through—

CHAPTER 19

"They're coming, Vinnie," Emily called. She was perched in the lowest branch of the elm tree in their front yard. Their house presented a sideways face to the road, so visitors to the cemetery were unlikely to notice her. She had been waiting in the tree for more than an hour.

Vinnie was at the front door, waiting for the signal. She went inside to distract their mother while Emily slithered down the tree and ran to the barn. She climbed the ladder to the hayloft and lay on her stomach near the wide window. Usually it was used to load hay into the barn for

Jasper and the other animals, but today it was her window on a funeral. Her brother's telescope lay at her side.

The sun was not yet at its zenith, but was steadily rising, bathing the cemetery in a light that put every blade of grass in sharp relief. The long shadows cast by the marble tombstones shortened steadily as the sun rose.

"It's a lovely day to say good-bye," Emily murmured. As if the deceased would care if the sun shone or if it rained! At moments like this, she hoped that her mother was right and that the good would find a place in heaven.

She put her eye to the telescope. Reverend Colton headed the procession. First to come was the coffin, carried by the sexton and his three sons. Behind them was Mrs. Langston, hanging heavily on Henry's arm. Then Ursula, carrying a demure bouquet and walking with an older man who resembled her and Henry. This must be their father, Charles Langston. Emily examined him with cynical eyes.

Charles Langston dressed well, like the rest of the family, but a shade too fancily for Amherst. He had dark hair, but Emily could make out a bald spot on the top of his head that he had carefully combed over. More interesting was a bruise on his right cheek. Dr. Gridley had mentioned that James's corpse had cuts on his right fist.

"I'll wager every book I own that you settled an account with Mr. Langston," she told the absent James. "I'm glad you hit him . . . but did it get you killed?"

Bringing up the rear was Sam Wentworth, looking smaller than the day before, as if his confessions at the brook had shrunk him.

The procession arrived at the freshly dug grave. Emily approved of the sexton's choice of gravesite, as she had a clear view from her vantage point.

"Can you see?" Emily started at Vinnie's unexpected voice. Vinnie had climbed the ladder, and her head popped up like a chipmunk. "Mother is fast asleep. What can you see?"

"Shhh," Emily said. Vinnie made a face and descended to the barn floor. She focused the telescope on Henry, but his face was as shuttered as an empty house. The coffin was lowered into the ground and Reverend Colton began his eulogy.

Suddenly the reverend jumped out of her view. She pulled back from the eyepiece and blinked at the whole group, suddenly tiny in the distance. They were rushing to Sam, who was clutching his heart. Falling heavily onto his knees, he reached toward Ursula and her mother. Violet Langston began screaming. Emily could faintly hear the words. "His medicine! Ursula, where are Samuel's pills?"

Ursula fumbled at her purse. She found a vial and, trembling, poured several pills into her mother's hands. Violet Langston gave them one at a time to Sam.

Transfixed, Emily watched, leaning out the window toward the scene. After a moment, Sam sat back on the grass and seemed to be breathing easier. Emily exhaled, too, and only then realized she had been holding her breath.

"Emily, what's going on?" Vinnie called up from the barn a few minutes later. "I can't see from down here."

"Sam had a bad turn," Emily answered. "His heart, I think."

"Is he all right now?"

"I think so. Ursula gave him his medicine. His color is much better."

"Ursula's mother said that she recently began making her uncle's heart medicine."

Vinnie's words sparked a fuse in Emily's brain.

When Emily didn't respond, Vinnie asked again, "Emily, what's happening?"

The new idea firmly lodged in Emily's mind, she lifted the telescope to her eye again. "It looks as though Henry is taking Sam home. The rest of the family is leaving."

"Mary Katherine told me that they are having lunch at the Amherst House with Reverend Colton."

Emily looked up from the telescope and stared at the beams above her head. "How on earth does Mary Katherine know that?" she asked slowly.

"Her sister, Bridget, works for the Langstons."

"Why didn't you tell me?" Emily asked, trying to keep the exasperation from her voice.

"Bridget just began to work there, but she said that the family is packing to go to Europe. She's upset that she already needs to find a new position."

Henry had said he would take his family away. "When are they going?" Emily called.

"Within a week."

"So we don't have much time."

"Father comes back in a few days. Your time is running out anyway."

Emily clambered down the ladder, the telescope under her arm. She shoved it at her sister. "Are you sure they're going to be at the hotel?"

Vinnie nodded.

"Then I need to get into the Langstons' house. Will Bridget be there today?"

"I think so." Vinnie's eyes were full of apprehension.

"That will be useful."

"To us." Vinnie's voice faltered. "I won't let you do this by yourself."

Emily hugged her little sister. "My darling, I'll do this alone, but you can keep lookout for me. If they return early, you can whistle like a . . . bobolink!"

Vinnie laughed nervously. "I don't know what a bobolink sounds like."

Emily briefly considered how to teach the complicated birdsong. "Never mind. We'll make it a crow. I know you can caw!"

The Langstons' house was located on the far side of the College, where many professors lived. The white house was Georgian in style, with an ostentatious garden. Emily shook her head; not one interesting plant in the bunch, although she had to admit the foxgloves and bleeding hearts were beautifully tall and full of blossoms. Emily stationed Vinnie behind an elm tree near the house with a good view of the street.

"Stay here and signal if you see the Langstons returning."

Vinnie nodded and as Emily walked up to the house, she could hear her sister practicing a crow's caw. "Only caw if you see them!" Emily reminded her.

Vinnie looked startled and then nodded with her finger to her lips.

Emily knocked on the front door. The girl with a wild mane of black hair who opened it could only be Mary Katherine's sister.

"Bridget?" Emily asked. "I'm . . . "

"Miss Emily Dickinson. Mary Katherine pointed you out to me." Bridget smiled, and Emily could see the gaps in her front teeth. "The family is at the cemetery, Miss."

"I know. I just came from there," Emily said.

"How can you bear to live so close to a graveyard?" Bridget asked. "Did you know that if you stumble in a cemetery it's a bad omen?"

Yes, this was Mary Katherine's sister, Emily thought. "Ursula—Miss Langston asked me to come and look for something." She felt guilty lying to Bridget, but it was the easiest way to get into the house.

"Of course, Miss Emily." Bridget stepped back to let her enter.

"Do you like working for the Langstons?" Emily asked. It was an indiscreet question, but she was curious.

Bridget shut the door and whispered, "They're the meanest family on the face of the earth. Nothing's good enough for Mrs. Langston. And that daughter—all she does is make messes for me to clean up. And never so much as a thank-you."

Emily made a sympathetic noise.

"What do you need to see, Miss?"

"Ursula's herbarium."

"Her what?" Bridget's thick eyebrows lifted in a questioning look.

"A large leather book that she presses flowers into."

"Oh, that!" Bridget brightened. "She's always working on it."

"Really?" Emily said. "Even since school ended?"

The maid shrugged. "She had it out this week. It's in the flower room."

"May I see?"

Bridget led the way through a house full of new furniture. Everything was ornate and to Emily's austere tastes, a little overblown, much like the flowers in the garden.

They walked down a long hallway into the flower room, which connected to the outside garden. It was a small room with a table and an assortment of vases and scissors. A good-sized window let in abundant light. Jars of dark liquids lined the shelves, and a wooden mortar and pestle were placed conveniently at hand.

"Here's the book, Miss," Bridget said, pushing it toward Emily.

Emily began flipping its pages, pausing to admire Ursula's neat penmanship and the superb organization of her pressed flowers. They were grouped by species, with careful notes. She found the page with foxgloves and read Ursula's notes avidly.

Bridget looked over her shoulder. "Those are those same flowers next to the front door. She cuts them all the time and works with them in here."

"What does she do with them?" Emily asked, although she was reading clear lists of instructions.

"She dries them and makes them into pills for Mr. Wentworth's heart."

The sound of a bird outside, an eager crow, reminded Emily that she was trespassing. "I must go, Bridget. May I leave through the back?"

"Of course. Follow me." Bridget held open the back door into the garden. As Emily slipped out, she came face to face with Horace Goodman, carrying a load of firewood to the kitchen.

"You're the girl from the tavern," he gasped. "What are you doing here?" His eyes darted around as though he wanted to flee, but the weight of the firewood kept him rooted to the spot.

Emily had no time to waste on calming words. "Give me Mr.—James Wentworth's things."

The caw of the crow grew more frantic.

Horace dropped the wood, just missing Emily's boots. "What things?"

"Horace, I know you gave the family your clothes to dress the body. I want to see the clothes he was wearing before."

"I didn't hurt him," Horace whispered.

"I know," Emily said. "But I can't help you unless you do as I say. Hurry."

Horace turned and half-ran to a shed attached to the barn. Emily followed on his heels, expecting to be discovered by an irate member of the Langston family at any minute.

Horace stepped inside the shed and brought out a bundle of clothes, which Emily spread on the ground. She recognized the dapper suit. In one of its pockets she found a familiar handkerchief with the initials "JW." She pulled it out, and a flask fell from its folds.

Vinnie's birdcall suddenly stopped. Emily stuffed the flask and handkerchief in her skirt pocket.

"Emily!" Vinnie's voice, deliberately cheerful, rang out. "Where are you? Look who I've met on the street. It's Mr. Henry Langston! Come here."

Emily peeked around the corner of the shed. Her sister and Henry were entering the garden at the far end. She still had a moment.

She turned to Horace. "Put the clothes away. Keep them in case they are needed." He silently nodded and gathered up the suit and shoes with his enormous hands.

"Emily!"

"I'm coming!" She ran back toward the house and found Vinnie chatting with Henry. He was smiling, but the cold appraisal he gave Emily told her that he was not fooled by Vinnie's prattling.

"Hello, Henry," Emily said, noting the knowing look on Vinnie's face at her familiar use of his first name.

"Emily. If I had known you wished to see our gardens so badly, I would have gladly shown them to you."

"Sometimes I just can't help myself," Emily said. "I just have to look at flowers."

Vinnie whispered loudly, "She has these turns. It's very worrisome."

"But I'm frightfully embarrassed to have come without permission," Emily said. "Please excuse the intrusion. Especially on such a sad day."

"Why aren't I surprised that you know about the funeral?" Henry narrowed his eyes and stared her down. "I thought we agreed that your investigation was done."

Glancing from Emily to Henry, Vinnie began to breathe faster.

"I never agreed," Emily said somberly. "I don't know exactly what caused James's death. Not yet."

Vinnie tucked her arm through Emily's and said brightly, "We must go home now; our mother is expecting us."

"The next time you wish to visit, please come when the family is at home and receiving," Henry said. "It would be more . . . prudent."

"Prudent?" Emily said coldly.

Vinnie's grip tightened on Emily's arm.

"I'd hate for you to waste your time," Henry said. "Life, as we have discovered, is fleeting."

"I'll keep that in mind." Emily's eyes met Henry's and held them until he looked away.

"Good-bye," Vinnie said, practically towing Emily toward the road. When they were out of earshot, she turned to her sister. "What did he mean about being prudent? Was he warning you?"

"Threatening me is more like it," Emily said.

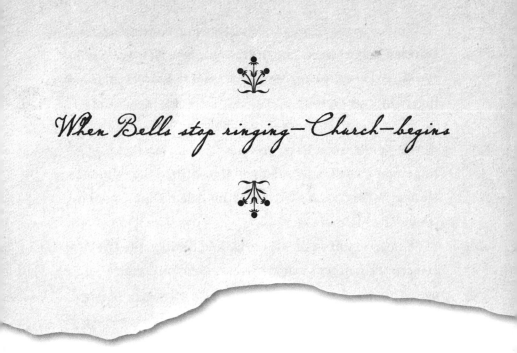

When Bells stop ringing—Church—begins

CHAPTER 20

"Hurry, Emily, we'll be late," Mrs. Dickinson scolded, draping a shawl over her shoulders.

Emily wrestled with a glove that was proving to be as rebellious as she felt. The last thing she wanted to do was to spend several hours in church—not when she was so close to answering all her questions.

"Emily, don't fuss so," Vinnie whispered in her ear. "All your suspects will be there."

"That's true," Emily admitted, as the glove suddenly capitulated and slipped onto her hand.

Vinnie's prediction proved accurate before they had traveled half a block. The first person she saw walking up the hill toward the church was Mr. Ripley. Emily hung back to let him catch her up.

"Mr. Ripley," she said. "Good morning."

He seemed ill at ease, and his complexion had a green tinge that made her wonder whether he had the influenza. He acknowledged her with a nod, his Adam's apple bobbing convulsively.

"I have very little time," Emily told him, keeping a sharp eye on her mother's back. "So let me assure you: I know everything."

"What?" he gulped. "You can't possibly . . ."

"The Langstons. The false codicil. Your bribe."

His eyes bulged. "So it *was* you! I saw that the blotting paper was missing the next day, but I couldn't bring myself to believe that a half-mad young girl . . . "

"Trust me, Mr. Ripley, the reports of my instability are greatly exaggerated," Emily said. "Yes, I took the blotting paper. But even more damning for your case, I have the original."

"But how?"

"Never mind. Your true dilemma lies before you: Do you confess everything you've done to my father, or do *I* tell him?"

He stopped in his tracks. "I can't. I would lose my position."

"Mr. Ripley, you are in danger of losing your liberty," Emily said flatly. "You could be prosecuted for fraud, if not worse!"

"Worse?" His voice rose an octave. A dozen paces ahead, Mrs. Dickinson's brisk step faltered for a moment, but she kept moving toward the church as though she were tied to the end of the rope that rang the bell calling the congregation to service.

"Conspiracy to commit murder," Emily said darkly.

"But I didn't do anything!" Mr. Ripley protested. "The Langstons swore to me he was dead. They told me the paperwork had gone astray in foreign parts. I believed them."

"Especially when they offered a generous fee?" Emily's voice was implacable, as her father's would no doubt be.

"The fee was more than welcome—but more than an honest job was worth. I should have been more suspicious," Mr. Ripley admitted. "When Mr. Wentworth came to the office and I saw that he was alive . . . I tried to do the right thing. You saw my affidavit. I admitted everything so he could recover his money."

"I did see it. It's the only thing that might save you. My father returns from Boston tomorrow afternoon. Tell him everything and trust to his mercy."

Mr. Ripley swallowed hard and nodded. Without a word, he turned and walked in the direction he had come, toward home and, Emily hoped, possible redemption.

Emily quickened her own steps to walk abreast with Vinnie. "I think he's going to confess to Father," she whispered.

"That's a relief, to my mind," Vinnie said.

"To mine as well. This business of playing with people's lives is very upsetting," Emily said. "Who am I to threaten a man's livelihood and liberty?"

"You are my brave Emily, who is tireless in her pursuit of truth." Vinnie tucked her hand inside her sister's elbow. "Look. Dr. Gridley is back."

Dr. Gridley was waiting at the corner of Amity and South Pleasant streets. It was obvious to Emily that he was waiting for her. He greeted Mrs. Dickinson and asked to speak to Emily privately.

Mrs. Dickinson grudgingly granted her permission. "But I expect Emily to be at the service on time," she ordered.

Dr. Gridley led Emily toward the porch of Orr's Apothecary. "I hear that our body has a name."

Emily nodded. "James Wentworth. He's the nephew of the Langstons and Sam Wentworth."

"Did you receive my letter?"

"I did." Emily's thoughts were churning rapidly—she needed the doctor to answer a few questions before she told him the latest developments. "I, too, suspect poison.

In fact, I have a particular one in mind. What do you know about foxglove?"

"Foxglove?" He looked surprised. "It contains digitalis. It could easily stop a healthy young man's heart."

"Excellent," Emily said, rubbing her hands. "That fits very well with my idea." She instantly regretted the satisfaction in her tone. She must never forget that James was dead, and if she were correct in her assumptions, someone would be arrested for murder, perhaps this very day.

"I understand, my dear. Sometimes I'm so excited to make a clever diagnosis that I forget what it means to my patient." Dr. Gridley patted her arm. "So digitalis fits your theory? Well, it's simple to make—the plants are in every formal garden in town. I also use it for heart medicine. It stops a normal heart, but if someone's heart is beating too quickly, it can slow it down to a safe rate."

Emily caught her breath. Dr. Gridley had just given her the final clue.

"So if someone took digitalis for heart trouble," she said slowly, "he could drink a dose that would kill a healthy man?"

"With no ill effects," Dr. Gridley confirmed.

"And what if the healthy man suddenly saw everything in a greenish hue?"

"That's a symptom of digitalis poisoning," he said, excitement in his voice. "Are you certain of your facts?"

Emily nodded.

"Well," the doctor said, rubbing his hands. "It's easy to test for. I'll have a word with the authorities and perform the test immediately."

Emily paused and then told him the bad news. "James Wentworth was buried yesterday."

"Already? That's ridiculous! My examination wasn't complete. We'll have to exhume the body." Dr. Gridley looked as though he was about to seek out the constable.

Emily couldn't bear to think of her friend's body being violated again.

"Wait," she said, and her resolute voice stopped him in his tracks. "I might have another way." From her purse, she pulled out the flask and handkerchief.

"What is this?" Dr. Gridley asked.

"This flask belonged to James Wentworth. I have a witness who saw him drink from it just before the world turned green and he collapsed."

Dr. Gridley stared at her as though she possessed magical powers. "You have been busy, Miss Dickinson."

"More busy than you could possibly imagine," she said. "Look!" She opened the flask and poured a tiny amount of the liquid onto the handkerchief.

"Miss Dickinson, we'll need that!"

"There is plenty left—but see what I find on the linen?" She held out the handkerchief. Specks of leaves dotted the brownish stain.

Speechlessly, Dr. Gridley held out his hand to collect the handkerchief. He smelled it. "Elderberry wine. An unusually sweet drink for a young man."

"Especially when he . . . when most young men would prefer brandy," Emily said, recalling the aroma in the smithy's stable.

Dr. Gridley didn't notice her aside. Touching his finger to the handkerchief, he smelt the leaves and then tasted them gingerly. "Digitalis," he confirmed. "What a dastardly thing to do! You know, Miss Dickinson, I have to take this to the constable."

Nodding reluctantly, Emily said, "I know."

"He'll have some questions for you, I'm sure."

She stifled a groan, thinking of her mother's reaction.

Dr. Gridley let out an exclamation. "There's Constable Chapman now! Excuse me." He abandoned her, walking toward the church so rapidly that a man of lesser dignity would have been running. He met Reverend Colton on the steps of the church, under the wide portico. Standing to one side was the constable. Emily could not hear what was said, but she saw the doctor gesturing widely and speaking with passion. Her name must have been mentioned, because all three men glanced in her direction before their animated conversation began again.

Emily watched from a distance. She knew she should give the affidavit to the authorities, but she preferred to wait a day until her father returned. He would know what to do.

"Are you finally coming?" Mrs. Dickinson said at her shoulder. "Your secret investigation is not more important than going to church."

Emily wanted to disagree. To her, church was a cold and artificial place to worship God. Unsure of the depths of her own faith, she knew she felt it more deeply and with more clarity when she was out of doors. James Wentworth had understood that. Would he have preferred to worship along the banks of Amethyst Brook?

"I'm coming, Mother," she said dutifully.

Vinnie was waiting near the church steps. Emily ignored her questioning looks because she had just spied another set of late arrivals. Coming from College Avenue, the Langstons appeared in the same order in which they had attended the funeral: first Henry and his mother, then Mr. Langston, and finally Ursula. Even Horace Goodman was there. Emily knew he would enter the church by the same door, but would immediately go upstairs to the gallery, where the freed blacks sat.

Only Sam Wentworth was missing. She hoped he had recovered from his heart attack, and that his medicine had proved effective. It was a small comfort that the means used to kill her friend could also save a life.

Constable Chapman saw the Langstons, too, and beckoned them to him. They looked reluctant, but it was too late for them to reverse course. Reverend Colton seemed torn between wanting to hear this conversation and starting the service on time. He kept looking at his pocket watch and glancing inside the Meeting House, where his congregation was waiting.

Vinnie's keen eyes had seen it all. "You know what happened, don't you?"

"Almost," Emily said absently, watching the reluctant progress of the Langstons toward the law's representative.

"Who did it?" Vinnie said. "I hope it's not Henry."

Emily held up a hand to forestall her sister. "I need proof before I tell you."

"That's just cruel of you. Now that Dr. Gridley is back and is talking with the constable, it's no longer your responsibility."

"I've run out of time," Emily said resentfully. "It's so unfair."

"That's just prideful, Emily Elizabeth Dickinson!" Vinnie scolded.

"I beg your pardon?"

"The important thing is that your precious Mr. Nobody gets justice—not who obtains it for him."

Emily glared at her sister. Of course it mattered, she thought. "Mr. Nobody and I talked about our lives having a purpose. Getting justice for his murder is my life's meaning right now."

Mr. and Mrs. Langston were almost at the church door when Ursula broke away and walked rapidly around the corner of the church into the College grounds. Intent on the upcoming interview, none of her family members appeared to notice her departure.

Emily gave her sister a scant moment of attention. "Tell Mother I felt faint and went home," she said. And she set off to follow Ursula.

"Emily!" She heard Vinnie behind her. "What are you doing?"

"Getting my proof!"

For each beloved hour

Sharp pittances of years,

Bitter contested farthings

And coffers heaped with tears.

CHAPTER 21

Emily half-ran, keeping Ursula's gray dress in her sights. Emily's breath grew shallow in her chest. She coughed, and when she took her hand away from her mouth she saw specks of blood on her white glove. The truth she was chasing didn't frighten her as much as those drops of blood, but she forced herself to keep moving. Her weakness would not prevent her from catching a murderer.

Ursula detoured around the College dormitory and then made her way back to her house, which she entered by the front door. Emily snuck around back to the flower room.

Through the window, she saw Ursula shoving fragments of foxgloves into an old sack, to which she added the contents of a jar filled with oblong white tablets.

As though she sensed she was being watched, Ursula froze and glanced toward the window. Emily ducked behind a large lilac bush. A moment later, the back door banged open and Emily watched as Ursula ran to the shed next to the barn and hid the sack. Emily wondered if Ursula knew that was also Horace's hiding place.

Ursula returned to the house, adjusting her hair and fixing her bodice. Emily waited a moment, and then went to the front door and knocked.

"Miss Dickinson!" It was Bridget, her face full of consternation when she saw who was calling. "The young master gave me a talking-to something fierce after you were here yesterday. You can't come in now; Miss Ursula is here!"

"I know she is," Emily reassured her. "Announce me, please."

A moment later, a red-faced Bridget ushered Emily into the parlor. Ursula was perched on a settee, doing embroidery. She looked up, put aside her hoop, and stood to greet Emily.

"Good morning," she said. "I'm surprised to see you here. Shouldn't you be in church?"

"I could ask you the same thing," Emily said, watching her closely.

Ursula hesitated. Emily was sure she was contemplating a lie. Finally Ursula said, "I did accompany my parents and Henry to church, but as soon as I saw Reverend Colton, I felt a massive headache coming on. That man does boom so; it's like being in an artillery battle." She sat down, gesturing for Emily to join her. "But I'm sure you understand, being plagued by ill health yourself. I daresay you missed half of last term at Amherst Academy to nurse your coughs."

"Thank you for your concern," Emily said, nettled. She saw her bouts of illness as no one's business but her own.

"Can I offer you some elderberry wine?" Ursula asked.

The wine from James's flask was still sticky on Emily's glove. She hastily declined.

Ursula's eyes narrowed, but she said agreeably enough, "Then some tea." Without waiting for Emily to answer, she called Bridget and gave her the order.

"I'm sorry to intrude at what must be a time of terrible grief," Emily said. Ursula's face was as blank as the next piece of paper in Emily's notebook. "Your cousin's death?" Emily prompted.

"Why, yes, I didn't realize that was general knowledge," Ursula said. "It was very sad. He drowned."

"I'm afraid that's not true," Emily said offhandedly, as if it weren't of the most vital importance.

"I beg your pardon?" Ursula said. Emily could see unease come into her pretty amber eyes.

"It was made to look like he drowned, but in fact he died when his heart stopped."

"I'm surprised to hear you say that." Ursula's fingers tightened on her embroidery hoop. "No other members of my family, who surely are in a better position to know, have said so."

"Your family is exceedingly good at keeping secrets from one another," Emily mused. "Much better than mine. My mother always seems to know everything, and Vinnie seems to have a sixth sense whenever I'm doing something I'd rather do alone. I expect she'll follow me here in a minute."

Ursula opened her mouth to speak but was forestalled by the arrival of Bridget with a tray. "Leave it here," Ursula said. "I'll pour." She turned her back to Emily and fussed with the cups. "Sugar?" she asked.

"Yes, please, one lump," Emily answered, trying to watch Ursula's hands.

Ursula handed Emily a cup. "Let us say you are right and Cousin James's heart stopped. The authorities would consider it a natural death. Why don't you?"

"I met your cousin, and I liked him very much. He didn't deserve what happened to him." Emily paused. "And as for the authorities, I think they are becoming more knowledgeable every minute."

There was a long silence while Ursula took a sip of tea. She seemed unconcerned, but her cup trembled. "And what knowledge do you think they are acquiring?" Her voice was tight.

"That you filled your cousin's flask with elderberry wine. A cousinly gesture. But what he didn't know was that the wine was laced with your uncle's heart medication."

"That's not true," Ursula protested weakly.

"You used the medication you made from the foxgloves in your own garden," Emily said. "Shame on you, Ursula, for using your healing skills to kill."

"I didn't," Ursula said in a tense voice. "Do you have any proof of this ridiculous accusation?"

Emily lifted her cup to her lips, deciding how much information to reveal. She looked over its rim at Ursula, who was watching her avidly. Without drinking, Emily deliberately returned her cup to its saucer.

"Proof enough," Emily said. "I have the flask filled with wine you gave him. There are still bits of foxglove floating in it."

Ursula was still.

"Not compelling enough? I have an eyewitness who saw James drink from it and then complain that the world around him had turned green. Dr. Gridley . . ." Ursula looked alert at the mention of the doctor's name. "He tells me that this is a symptom of foxglove poisoning."

"A tragic mistake," Ursula said. "Somehow my uncle's medicine got into the wine."

"Into the flask that you filled? Under what circumstances could that have happened? And if that was the case, then why did you just hide the foxglove and the pills in your back shed?"

Ursula's eyes darted in the direction of the shed. With an obvious effort she brought her gaze back to the tea tray. She checked the pot of tea, acting the polite hostess in a way that Emily found more unnerving than if Ursula had gone into hysterics.

"You haven't drunk your tea, Emily," she said. "Is it not to your liking?"

"It's fine. A little hot, perhaps," Emily said, playing along as an honored guest.

There was a long silence, finally broken when Ursula asked, "Surely you aren't suggesting that I somehow transported my cousin into your pond?"

"Oh no, I don't think that at all," Emily assured her. "That was when your murder got tangled up with other people's attempts to cover up their crimes."

"I don't understand what you're saying."

Emily thought that was probably true. "Your Uncle Sam and your hired man put James's body in the pond. But your parents were complicit. It was their idea to change James's clothes so that he looked more like a hired hand than a member of the family. None of them could afford any questions about a living heir to the fortune they had already stolen—excuse me, arranged to inherit themselves."

Ursula stared, shocked. Emily was certain that this was the first she had heard of the aftermath of her cousin's death. This was a secretive family indeed.

"It must have been so confusing for you," Emily mused, "when James's body wasn't found. And then for it not to be identified. Through a wild stroke of fortune, you must have thought you had gotten away with it."

"I don't know what you mean," Ursula said. "You are talking more nonsense than you usually do." She stood up and approached Emily. "Your tea must be cold. Let me pour you another."

Without a word, Emily handed Ursula her untouched cup.

"But why did you do it?" Emily said. "Was it just for the money?" She couldn't help it, but her voice reflected her disdain for such a base motive.

"Just the money?" Ursula asked bitterly, still holding Emily's cup. She went to the window and stared unseeingly into the ornate garden. "The mighty Dickinsons don't know what it's like not to have money. And even if you were poor, with your history and education, you would still be accepted in this town. The founders of Amherst College! You have everything. Without that money, we had nothing."

Suddenly the door flew open, Henry, his tie askew and his face red with running, burst in. Vinnie followed close on his heels. Henry's eyes went first to Emily and then to his sister.

"Emily," he said, panting. "Are you all right?"

"Of course," she said. She hesitated, knowing that she was about to bring ruin to Henry's family. "I was just telling Ursula that I've given Dr. Gridley the proof that she poisoned her cousin. No doubt he and the constable are interviewing your parents right now."

"Your sister told me about Gridley and the constable." Henry didn't take his eyes off Ursula. "Suddenly I understood what happened to Cousin James."

"I think perhaps you always suspected it," Emily said softly.

"I feared it." He went to his sister and took her hands. "Ursula, you've done such a wicked thing. Why?"

"It was all that money." Her eyes were unfocused, and she spoke in fits and starts. "Before we inheriited the money, everything was going wrong. Father's business failed. You had to leave Yale. The dressmakers wouldn't give me credit anymore. Mother said we would have to move in with Uncle Samuel in that smelly old house. I wouldn't have been able to go to school. That money meant my life."

"Your parents stole it from James," Emily said.

"So?" Ursula retorted. "He didn't need it—and we did."

"How could you bear to profit from a lie?" Vinnie asked. Ursula stared at her, as though she was noticing her arrival for the first time.

"If you can resist taking everything you've ever wanted, then you can sneer at me," Ursula said with a snarl.

"But to kill, Ursy?" Tears ran down Henry's cheeks. "James was family."

Ursula didn't say anything, but she twisted the rings on her long fingers as though her life depended on it.

"The worst thing of all is that it wasn't necessary," Emily said sadly. "James wasn't going to prosecute. He didn't even want the money back. You did it all for nothing."

The color drained from Ursula's face. "You're lying," she spat. "At school you always thought you were better than me. Smarter. I won't let you fool me."

"It's true, Ursy," Henry said, rubbing his cheek with the back of his hand.

Ursula staggered away from her brother, grabbing the back of a chair to steady herself. She stared at Emily with cold eyes. "I was always jealous of you. But maybe not so much now."

"Why not?" Emily said warily.

"Because you will have to live with this, and I will not." Ursula grabbed the teacup that had been Emily's. Before anyone could stop her, she gulped the contents.

"Henry, there's poison in the cup!" Emily cried.

"Ursula!" he shouted. He rushed to his sister and she clung to his arms. He carried her to the sofa and laid her down.

"Henry, I'm so sorry," Ursula said.

Vinnie began to sob. Emily held her tightly, hiding her sister's eyes from what was happening.

"Everything is green . . ." Ursula said. Then she slumped into her brother's arms.

"Fetch the doctor," he cried.

Vinnie, relieved to be of use, said, "I'll go!"

"It won't matter," Emily said. "Ursula knew how much to dose the tea."

Vinnie flashed her a stricken look. "Emily!"

"Go, Vinnie; fetch Dr. Gridley," Emily said. "But it's already too late. Death won't wait for him."

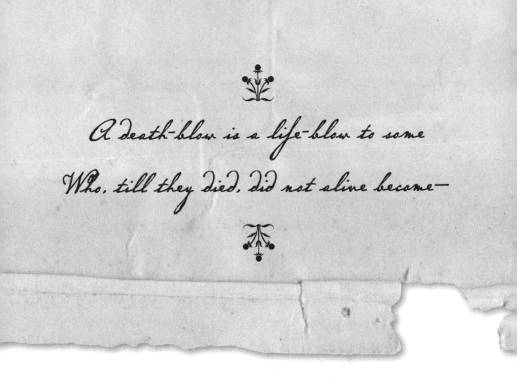

A death-blow is a life-blow to some
Who, till they died, did not alive become—

EPILOGUE

Emily retreated to her room for several days with only Vinnie and a succession of cats for company. By the time she emerged, her father had returned. He lectured Emily about taking risks. For once, she didn't resent his warnings. Life continued at the Dickinson home as though James Wentworth had never existed—or been murdered.

Shortly afterwards, Emily received a note from Henry. He wrote that he was about to leave town and begged to speak to her before his departure.

She met him in front of the stagecoach stop at the Amherst House Hotel in the center of town and sat on a bench on the hotel's second-floor veranda.

At first their conversation was about his journey. The coach would take him to Northampton, where he would board a train to New Haven. Travel in the summer was often dusty. He might break his journey in Hartford.

Without warning, Henry asked, "Did you know my sister would try to kill you?"

Emily sighed with relief that they were finally talking about things that mattered. "I did wonder," she said. "Especially after she offered me elderberry wine. And then she was so insistent that I drink the tea. Of course, I never had any intention of drinking anything she might give me."

"It is so hard to believe that my own sister could do such a thing."

"Reverend Colton warned me that if someone has killed, he is even more dangerous afterward. He—or she—will always see murder as a solution again."

"My own sister," he repeated.

Neither said anything. Finally, Emily began to speak. "Horace has been cleared of any wrongdoing. The authorities seem to think he is simple; he was just following orders."

Henry remained silent.

"My father has dismissed Mr. Ripley but has declined to prosecute him," she continued. "Father says that Mr. Ripley was just greedy and weak-minded. Not criminally culpable like . . ."

"My parents?" Henry supplied.

Emily shrugged. It was a fact. "What will happen to them?" she asked.

"My father has taken full responsibility for the fraud. He will probably go to prison for some time. My mother is moving back to Boston to be with her family."

"I'm sure they will offer her the solace she needs," Emily said politely.

"And what does your father have to say about your investigations?"

"He's pretending that I had nothing to do with solving your cousin's death. My mother, as always, toes whatever line my father draws." Emily paused, not liking the bitterness in her own voice. "The important thing is that justice was done."

"I suppose," Henry said, although Emily suspected his heart wasn't in it.

"And you?" she asked. "Will you go back to school as though nothing has happened?"

"I've written to the president of the university, and he agrees that for now it's the best plan. You see, I didn't know anything until after the fact."

Emily nodded. "And once you did, you were in an impossible position. How can you expose a criminal who's a member of your own family?"

"What would you have done?" Henry asked.

"I don't know," Emily admitted. "I love each member of my family so dearly that I think it would kill me to make that choice."

"I pray to God you never have to."

They were silent, watching the townspeople below go about their business. The stagecoach arrived from Northampton and the driver jumped down to water the horses for the return trip. They didn't have much time.

"What will happen to James's fortune?" Emily asked.

"My mother has forfeited her right to inherit," Henry said. "So it comes to Sam and me."

"Convenient," Emily said drily.

"If I refuse it," Henry defended himself, "then it goes to the state. How does that help anyone? I'll need it to begin a new life and have a career untainted by my family's crimes."

"I think people can convince themselves of the right in anything they truly want," Emily retorted.

Henry would not meet her eyes. He stood up and walked to the porch railing and looked out over the Common,

MICHAELA MacCOLL

where cows grazed placidly. He turned to face Emily again. "Ursula's body will be sent back to Boston to be buried there," he said. "In Mount Auburn."

"Very prestigious," Emily said.

He opened his mouth to say something and thought better of it. After a minute he seemed to gather himself. "Emily, I wanted to ask you . . . I have no right, but I felt I must. . . . My father's shame is public, and his reputation is beyond repair."

Emily nodded.

"But very few outside the family know of Ursula's crime. Only the constable, Dr. Gridley, your sister, and yourself."

Emily felt a cold block of cynicism settle in her stomach. "And?"

He sat down on the bench next to her and took her hand. "Surely there's no need to add to my mother's burden by proclaiming what my sister did."

"You want me to remain silent." Emily's voice flattened. She tried to pull her hand away.

"If you would. I know it is much to ask." His hand squeezed hers tightly.

"And your cousin James? Doesn't he deserve the truth?"

"Ursula was your friend," he said. "You barely knew James!"

Emily started as though Henry had struck her.

"Or was there more to your friendship than I know?" He stared at her, suspicion in his eyes.

Emily sighed. "We talked for only a few minutes. Less than an hour, all told."

"Then what can it matter to you? You are kind and good, Emily. Grant my family this one grace. My sister is dead—what use is it to talk about what happened?" He hesitated. "Please, do it for me. Think of my career. How can I succeed with this millstone around my neck?"

Suddenly Emily felt a wave of revulsion. She was sick of it all.

"Of course, Mr. Langston. I have no interest in gossiping about this dreadful affair." She stood up and straightened her skirt. "Good-bye. I trust we shall not meet again."

"Good-bye, Miss Dickinson."

As Emily walked away from the hotel, she thought about Henry Langston's plea for discretion. To whom did she owe the truth? To the dead or to the living?

"James Wentworth had decided to forgive his family," she said aloud. "I'll respect his wishes. If I'm asked about the events of this week, I can be honest without being cruel." Her decision made, she pulled out her notebook.

Tell all the truth, but tell it slant.

She skirted her home and climbed the gentle hill to the cemetery. She cut across the grassy expanse dotted with

MICHAELA MACCOLL

graves, unerringly heading for Mr. Nobody's resting place. The earth was still too unsettled for a tombstone; the spot was marked by a wooden cross and Ursula's wilted bouquet. The cemetery was quiet, save for the lonely cawing of a single crow.

She flipped the pages of her notebook until she found the secret jotting she had made the day she and Mr. Nobody had met. It wasn't very long—only twelve short lines, and she couldn't swear that her punctuation and spelling were flawless. She carefully tore the page from its binding, folded it in quarters, and tucked it in the dirt under the flowers.

It was a poem about meeting a stranger who became a friend and ally. His name was Nobody, and it was meant only for eyes that were closed forever. Then she laid a posy of rosemary on the freshly turned dirt. Rosemary, for remembrance.

Emily looked across the cemetery. The afternoon sun bathed her white house in a gentle light. In the shadow of the great elm, Vinnie was waiting for her. Emily ran down the slope to the warmth and safety of Home.

I'm nobody!

Are you

Then there's

They'd

How dreary

How public

To tell your name—

Who are you?

nobody too?

a pair of us—don't tell!

banish us, you know!

to be somebody!

like a frog—

the linelong day—

To an admiring bog!

Author's Note

At the age of twelve, I discovered Emily Dickinson's poetry and was hooked. In particular I remember the poem that began, "This is my letter to the World/That never wrote to Me." I'll never forget that moment of recognition that Emily and I saw things the same way. My experience relating to her poetry isn't unique. Emily Dickinson is considered one of America's greatest and most popular poets. She had an ability to describe the world around her with originality, honesty, humor, and passion, and without sentimentality.

Fewer than a dozen of Emily's poems were published during her lifetime. And those that were published weren't popular, as many people couldn't see past her odd spelling and unique punctuation (for instance, she used dashes frequently in place of standard periods or commas). Today, these elements are part of what people love about her poetry—to the twenty-first-century reader, her punctuation feels fresh and modern.

Emily's poems inspired this story, especially "I'm Nobody! Who are You?," which is about how enticing anonymity might be in a small town where everyone knows everyone else's business. The first chapter is all about bees because bees feature in more than fifty of her poems. She was also intrigued by death, loss, and loneliness. That her poems portrayed so much—and such varied—emotion made the task of choosing a poem to reflect the emotional content of each chapter of my book surprisingly easy.

Emily's powerful poetry is all the more extraordinary given how quiet her life was. Born in 1830, she lived her entire life in Amherst, Massachusetts, except for one year of school in South Hadley, only ten miles away. She died at the age of fifty-five from liver disease in the house where she lived most of her life.

The one surviving photograph of Emily Dickinson was considered a poor likeness; it was too plain and severe. Small wonder that she preferred to craft her own self-portrait in words. She wrote, "I am small, like the Wren, and my Hair is bold, like the chestnut bur, and my eyes like the Sherry in the Glass, that the Guest leaves."

Emily was the middle child between her brother, Austin, and her sister, Lavinia ("Vinnie"). Austin was her closest confidant, and she missed him terribly when he went away to school. The sisters were close, but very different. While Emily was partial to birds, Vinnie preferred cats. Vinnie was the more vivacious of the two. Young men from Amherst seemed to prefer flirting with Vinnie, but Emily was the one they preferred to talk to.

Emily's father, Edward, was a successful lawyer, politician, and an official of Amherst College. Although he educated his daughters, there was no question of their becoming "literary." Girls in the nineteenth century (and well into the twentieth) were expected to manage the responsibilities of a household. As Emily tells Mr. Nobody, her father bought her books, but discouraged her from reading them in case they put ideas in her head. Please note that the letter in the novel from Mr. Dickinson is fictional, although typical of the way he wrote to his family.

Her mother, Emily Norcross Dickinson, was far less concerned with Emily's education than with her poor health. She also worried about the family finances, particularly since her father-in-law had spent the family fortune to found Amherst College. Mrs. Dickinson always claimed that Mrs. Child's *The American Frugal Housewife* had enabled her to make ends meet, and often quoted it to her exasperated daughters.

For eight years, Emily attended Amherst Academy, where she studied botany with Almira Lincoln Phelps, one of the most notable botanists of the time. Miss Phelps encouraged Emily to keep a herbarium, a large book in which to keep her pressed flowers and plants. Unusually, the girls at the academy were permitted to attend lectures by the most distinguished scholars of the day at the all-male Amherst College. Emily's poems are filled with references to her study of chemistry, astronomy, and geology.

Although she had suitors, Emily never married. She remained in her family home, caring for her parents and the house. She hated housework, calling it a "pestilence," although she enjoyed the chemical combustion involved in baking. Her recipes won prizes at a local fair.

In my novel, I tried to show how time-consuming and tedious cooking was for Emily and her sister. Research indicates that Emily increased her output of poems whenever the family had full-time help, and dropped off when they didn't.

Since Emily spent so much time in the kitchen, many of her poems were written there, jotted down on any scrap of paper, even the backs of bills and advertisements. Eventually she transferred her poems, which often had many versions, to handmade books made of folded paper and fastened with string, called fascicles. Though there is no evidence that she kept such a notebook hidden in her corset as she does in the novel, it seemed plausible to me.

Some of Emily's fascicles have been preserved, and may be seen at the Emily Dickinson Museum in Amherst. The museum is located in the Homestead, her family home. She was born there, but financial troubles forced the Dickinsons to leave the house when she was nine. They moved to a house on North Pleasant Street, adjoining the cemetery. The family lived there until Emily's father managed to repurchase the Homestead when Emily was twenty-five.

My story takes place during the time they lived on North Pleasant Street. Emily is now buried in the cemetery she could see from her bedroom window. Unfortunately, this house is long gone and has been replaced by a gas station, but pictures of it still exist.

The gentlemen Emily enlists as allies, Reverend Colton and Dr. Gridley, were close friends of the Dickinson family, but the Wentworths and the Langstons are pure invention.

As a teenager, Emily had an active social life in Amherst. She went to teas, sewing circles, fairs, and sleigh rides with friends. Far from avoiding society, as she did later in life, as a teen she longed for it and stayed home only to nurse her ill mother. The scene where Henry surprises Emily in the kitchen was inspired by a letter she wrote to a friend complaining that she could not go riding with a dear friend because her mother was ill.

She wrote, "A friend I love so dearly came and asked me to ride in the woods, the sweet-still woods . . . I told him I could not go . . ."

Then she wrote, "I went cheerfully round my work, humming a little air till mother had gone to sleep, then cried with all my might."

Emily's schoolfriends could not keep up with the fierce intelligence she expressed in her letters to them. As she entered her twenties, her social circle shrank to the family and very close family friends. However, she expanded her correspondence to include some of the great thinkers of the time.

By the time Emily was thirty, she had become a recluse, rarely leaving her home, and she wore only white cotton housedresses. Because they rarely saw her, the townspeople began to refer to her as "Myth" or the "Woman in White."

A few of her poems were published in local newspapers without her permission. Emily was furious that her punctuation and spelling had been "corrected" and refused to consider publishing again, although she shared many of her poems with family and friends. Yet no one in her limited circle suspected how much she was writing.

After Emily's death, Vinnie was shocked to find more than 1,800 poems among Emily's things. Always her sister's champion, she arranged for them to be published. Emily would have been dismayed to see that the editors once again altered her punctuation, titled her poems, and even changed words to improve the rhymes. But she might have smiled to see that the cover was illustrated with Indian pipes, her favorite flower.

Despite the editors' meddling, the poems were a critical and commercial success, establishing Emily as a major poet. It was not until 1955 that her original poems, exactly as she wrote them, were published in a comprehensive collection. The poems quoted at the beginning of each chapter and the excerpts in chapters 5 and 13 are excerpts from that first edition of Emily's work which may not always reflect Emily's creative intent. However, they are in the public domain so they can be used freely here. "I'm Nobody, Who are You?" is quoted in its entirety. However the clues that Emily writes down in her secret notebook are fictional. Likewise Mr. Nobody did not exist and Emily Dickinson never investigated a murder.

The town of Amherst still resembles the town Emily knew. I took all the walks that Emily took—Amethyst Brook is a walk of a few miles out of town, and I, too, found Indian pipes along its banks.

FURTHER READING

If you are interested in Emily Dickinson, read her poetry! The poems are easily found online, and there are many collections available in your library.

The most comprehensive is *The Complete Poems of Emily Dickinson,* edited by Thomas H. Johnson (Little Brown, 1960).

My favorite biography is *My Wars Are Laid Away in Books: The Life of Emily Dickinson* by Alfred Habegger (Modern Library, 2002). A wonderful pictorial biography is *The World of Emily Dickinson* by Polly Longsworth (W.W. Norton, 1997).

I also recommend a visit to the Emily Dickinson Museum. If you can't go in person, it has a terrific website: http://www.emilydickinsonmuseum.org/. It is full of interesting information and a "Poem of the Week."

Another useful online location is the Amherst Public Library's digital Emily Dickinson collection, http://www .joneslibrary.org/specialcollections/collections/dickin son/dickinson—print.html. You can see her shopping lists and samples of her poems. The library also has a wonderful digital collection about Amherst through the years at http://www.digitalamherst.org.

Nobody's Secret

1. The young man who Emily calls Mr. Nobody tells her, "I'm nobody important." Why do you think he describes himself this way? How does his anonymity ultimately drive Emily forward in her quest to learn more about him?

2. What is it about Mr. Nobody that catches Emily's attention from their very first encounter? Do you think he is equally taken by her? Why or why not?

3. Describe Emily's relationship with her sister, Vinnie. How are these two girls similar to each other? How are they different? Do you believe them to be close? Why or why not?

4. While discussing the possibility of her being stung by a bee, Emily tells Mr. Nobody, "It's a new experience. If you are sequestered at home, as I am, new experiences are to be savored." What are the ways Emily copes with her lack of freedom? Given what you've learned about her family, do you think her approach is the right one? Why or why not?

5. Consider the lines from Emily Dickinson's poetry that are used to introduce the chapters; how do her words help set the tone for the story? Did you have a particular favorite or one you enjoyed most?

6. The Dickinson's family home sits next to a graveyard, which Emily considers one of the house's assets. How would you feel about living close to a graveyard? What is it about these "neighbors" that she appreciates?

7. Emily's mother is described as ignoring larger issues and fixating on highly unusual calamities, as well as her own personal health. Consider Mrs. Dickinson's condition; though medical diagnoses are greatly different now than they were during her lifetime, what type of medical condition do you suspect she suffered from?

8. Why do you think Emily feels so determined to solve the mystery of Mr. Nobody? Do you think the danger she puts herself and her sister in is justified? Why or why not?

9. When speaking about her family's very visible presence at church, Emily states, "Wouldn't it be lovely if we could worship wherever we wished?" Why do you think she feels that way? Have you ever had a similar sense of obligation that stemmed from your family's expectation? What makes this so challenging?

10. Consider the visit of Ursula Langston and her mother to the Sewing Circle held at the home of the Dickinsons. Why is Mrs. Langston's behavior deemed so inappropriate? In what ways does her daughter try to censor her mother? Have you ever been in a similar position with a family member or friend? What did you do to deal with the situation?

11. After getting confirmation of her involvement in their cousin's murder, Henry tells his sister, "Ursula, you've done such a wicked thing." Do you think Henry is sincere in his profession to Ursula? Do you think he and the rest of the family should share the blame for James's death? Why or why not?

For more book club guides, visit
www.chroniclebooks.com/teen.

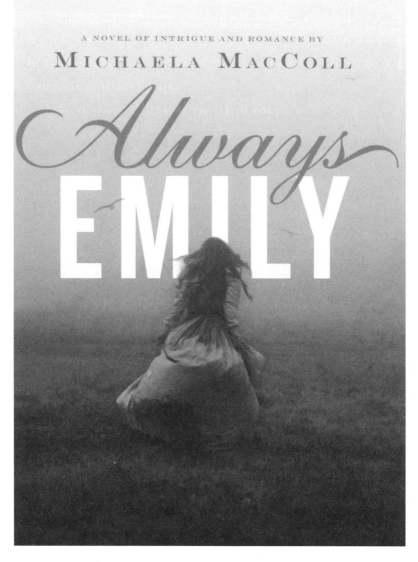

A NOVEL OF INTRIGUE AND ROMANCE BY

MICHAELA MacCOLL

Always
EMILY

Available wherever books are sold.
For more distinctive books for teens,
visit chroniclebooks.com/teen.

A Sneak Peek at

a NEW Novel of Intrigue and Romance

ALWAYS EMILY
BY MICHAELA MACCOLL

CHAPTER ONE

August 1835

How much farther?" Emily asked. Her long body pressed into the corner of the carriage seat, as if she were trying to propel herself back home toward Haworth.

"A mile less than the last time you asked," Charlotte said between gritted teeth. She sat primly in the corner, her feet barely touching the floor. Charlotte tried to make up for her lack of inches with perfect posture. A notebook and pen were at hand, but Charlotte hadn't written a single word. Emily had proved to be a distraction as a traveling companion.

"You didn't tell me this school was so far away," Emily said, staring out the dirty window. "I never would have agreed to go."

"You didn't agree," Charlotte pointed out. "Father insisted."

"Because you badgered him without respite."

"Badger?" Charlotte's hand went to her bodice. "I'm sorry if planning for the future is bothersome to you and Father."

Emily glared at her sister with raised eyebrows. Suddenly she tugged the window open and stuck her head out.

"Em, close the window. Ladies don't thrust their heads out into the road. It's common."

"I don't care what anyone thinks." Emily shoved her body farther out the window. She recognized the landscape—they were near the great bog of Crow Hill. Charlotte had lied when she said they were making progress; they were barely ten miles from home. The landscape was still familiar. The great green hills were just starting to turn purple with the heather. In September, these hills would be heavy with the scent of the flowers and their vibrant color would swamp the eyes. But Emily wouldn't be there to see it.

On the horizon, beneath a row of fir trees stunted by the constant wind on the moors, Emily noticed a figure on horseback galloping across the top of a hill, the perfect symbol of the liberty she was giving up. Emily wanted to fix the memory of that rider in her mind. When she was locked up at school this anonymous figure would be her talisman; a promise that someday Emily would roam the moors again.

Suddenly her shoulder was gripped by a small hand and Emily was hauled inside. Charlotte, stumbling against the motion of the carriage, slammed the window shut. "The moors will still be there when you get home." She sat back down and crossed her arms.

"But how long will that be?" Emily said. "When you went to school, you stayed for two entire years."

"I came home for holidays." She patted Emily's leg. "And you will, too. You'll be home for Christmas."

"Four months!" Emily's voice was high and anxious. "How will I stand it?"

"I've told you time and time again—school is not a punishment. Father is a fine teacher, but at Roe Head School I learned things I never could have at the parsonage."

Emily's expression spoke eloquently of her doubts.

"Don't scowl at me like that, Emily. I've learned languages and geography and grammar. Your education has been too eccentric. If you're to earn a living, you must know the academic subjects as well as music, deportment, and the rest." Charlotte's words slipped glibly off her tongue from long repetition.

"I don't care about earning my living," Emily exclaimed. "No one wants me to work except you!"

"Look at me, Emily," Charlotte commanded. When Emily continued to stare out the window, Charlotte reached over and grabbed her sister's chin. "You're seventeen now, and we must face the facts of our situation. Father is our only bulwark against destitution. When he dies, we lose our income and our home. We must be prepared to support ourselves."

Emily batted Charlotte's hand away. "Your concern for the future keeps you imprisoned in the present. Why lock yourself up in a school when Father's healthy as an ox? You worry for nothing."

Charlotte's hand clenched and unclenched. "How can you forget his illness this past spring? We might have lost him then!" Her wide brown eyes filled with tears as she remembered those days nursing their father. It was then she'd formulated a plan to save the family. She would return to school, but as a teacher. Rather than a full salary, her recompense would include tuition for Emily. It was the perfect plan. Except for one thing. Emily.

"I have no interest in teaching or governessing." Emily spoke with deliberation. Charlotte had tried to arrange everything without consulting Emily, who would not soon forgive her sister for it.

"Would you prefer marriage?" Charlotte asked. "Because that's your only alternative." A snort was Emily's only response. Charlotte leaned back against the dusty cushion and closed her eyes. Melodrama was exhausting.

After another mile or so, Emily spoke in a softer voice. "What is this school like? Will I hate it?"

Charlotte opened her eyes and smiled. "You may like it very much. I made good friends there. You've met my friend Ellen. She's lovely, don't you agree?"

Emily tugged at the fingers of her darned gloves, picking at the ragged seams. "I suppose so."

"The days are filled with learning," Charlotte continued. "It's very well organized."

Emily's eyes filled with malice; she asked, "And how much writing did you do while you were there? Did the Adventures of Angria continue at Roe Head or did they shrivel wasted on the vine?"

Charlotte was silent.

"I seem to remember you writing frantically when you came home," Emily said.

"Miss Wooler, the headmistress, says we must bend our inclination to our duty. If necessary, I'll sacrifice my writing to earn security for my family," Charlotte muttered.

"Selflessness is your specialty, not mine," Emily retorted. "What if I am not willing to surrender my dreams?"

Charlotte glared at Emily, who had the grace to look abashed.

With her facility for logic that alternately impressed and infuriated Charlotte, Emily leapt to another argument. "If I have to go to school, why do I have to change the way I look?"

Emily ran her fingers across her scalp and bits of crimped hair broke off in her hands. "Look what your hairdressing did! I look absurd with curls."

Charlotte privately agreed Emily's fair coloring and light eyes were better suited to a less labored hairdressing, but she hastened to reassure her sister. "No, it's fashionable." She wrapped one of her dark ringlets around her finger. "I'm trying to spare you the mistakes I made. When I arrived at school, everyone made fun of my clothes and hair."

"What do I care about what people think?" Emily snapped her fingers with a loud snap, a habit Charlotte deplored because she couldn't do it.

"You're not in Haworth anymore," Charlotte said. "I'm trying to keep you from being lonely like I was at first."

Emily shot a glance at her sister. With an unfamiliar pang of guilt, she reached out and took Charlotte's hand. "You're trying to help me and I'm acting the shrew." After a moment, she added, "I'm out of my element and it's putting me out of sorts. Tell me more about the school so I know what to expect."

"The students take long walks, weather permitting. You'll like that."

"Weather permitting? I walk in any weather. The more wuthering the better." Stormy weather on the moors was called a wuthering and it was one of Emily's favorite words.

"We walk often enough," Charlotte said firmly. "Miss Wooler says it builds strong bodies and spurs the appetite.

The food is quite good—and unlike home, we don't have to do the washing up."

Emily looked sidelong at Charlotte. "It's not like . . . Cowan Bridge?" This was the question she had avoided asking ever since school had become inevitable. Two of their sisters had died at Cowan Bridge from cold and neglect.

"Of course not!" Charlotte contemplated her sister with pity. No wonder Emily was so obstinate about school; how could she have not seen it? "Cowan Bridge was an awful place. Father would never make that mistake again." Her voice contained a speck of blame for their father's carelessness. "And I'll be there with you. There's nothing to fear."

"You and I will share a room, won't we?" Emily asked.

Charlotte had dreaded this question. "You hate sharing a room with me!"

"But it would be a familiar irritation," Emily said.

"I'm to be a teacher, so I'll have my own room," Charlotte said, looking at Emily warily. "You'll be in the dormitory."

Emily straightened up and glared at Charlotte. "I have to share a room with strangers?"

Charlotte took a deep breath and delivered the worst news. "You'll share a bed with another student."

Emily's face was like stone.

"But in the winter, it's handy for the warmth," Charlotte hurried on. "And it's fun to have someone to whisper secrets with in the dark."

"My secrets are my own," Emily said flatly

The carriage slowed and turned onto a gravel drive. Emily abandoned Charlotte and studied the school as the carriage crunched up the incline. The building was large—three stories—and surrounded by giant oak and cedar trees.

"You didn't say it was so big," Emily whispered.

"Truly, Emily, it's a good school," Charlotte answered. "You could be happy here. If only you'll try."

The carriage shuddered to a stop. The driver hopped down from his perch atop the roof and opened the door. Charlotte, stiff from the ride, awkwardly climbed down. Emily jumped to the ground without using the step.

Staring up at the imposing wooden doors, Emily muttered, "I won't last a week."

"Nonsense," Charlotte said, her cheerful tone ringing ominously false. "Give it a month. By then you will have settled in and you won't want to be anywhere else."

As if they had a heft and weight, Emily pushed away her fears with a wave of her hand. "A month then, Charlotte." But in the privacy of her mind, Emily added, "After then, with or without you, I'm going home."